A
DAY IN
PARADISE

2

A
DAY IN
PARADISE
2

LEIGH MCKNIGHT

ISBN #978-1-7333013-5-0

www.mcknightdixcreations.weebly.com

DEDICATION

This book is dedicated to my parents
E. W. & Ruby Dix

ACKNOWLEDGEMENT

First, I thank the Lord for allowing me to continue on this literary journey that I love so much, as well as all of His many blessings.

Also, thanks to my family for their love and support; Dix, McKnight, Bookhardt, McKune, Williams, Turner, Reynolds, Bells, Bennett, Greer, Rembert, Favor, Henderson, Jenkins, Prince, Houck, Shuler, Dash, Murphy, Hamilton, Johnson, Gordon, Richburg, Fairey, Barnett, Fludd, Morton, Pendleton, Kennerly, Frederick, Clarkson and Zeigler.

I also Acknowledge two dear friends and wonderful editors; Celeste Brown and Angelina Daniels Shaw. Thanks also to Mirika M. Cornelius, Reggie & Crystal Bennett, Dm Lane, Velma Chandler, Tavi Lawson, Christine Robinson,

Katie F. Benedict, ML Witherspoon, Katherine S. Murphy, Mary Watson Morris, Pamela Davis, Ella Fludd, Selina Lawson, Jamia Parks, Carl & Shiann Owens, Tonya Golden, Ernestine Fairey, Francine Smiley, Brenda Jackson-McKnight, Mary Frasier, Okereta Watson, Edith Watson Canzater, Crystal Dawn Williams, Mary Rhim, Sonya B. Harvin, Barbara J. Wiley, Sharon G. Jones, Sonja Wilson-Murphy, Saundra Shuler, Dianne Barnes, Breslyn Pringle, Timmie Gibson, Author Mlbrooks, John & Sherry G. King, Josephine Holliday, Willie B. Holston, LaFonda Hayes, Tyora Moody, Lessie Watson Dawkins, LeAnn Pittman, Geniffer J. Bookhardt, Mickey Jolly, Wanda H. Moran, Gigi Armani, LouQueen Shuler, George & Fredia Hunt, Jometa Gordon, Darlene Montgomery, Darnetta McCray, Marilyn Frazier, Norine Phillips, Lisa Sowers, Margaret Johnson, Lynette Weeks, Luether Maple, Gussie Boatwright, Betty Porcher, Sue T. Nicks, Avis Stafford, Helena Kopczynski, Charlene Williams, Pauline Bogger, Yildiz M. Isik, Amaka I. Nkosazana, Hyacinth Kinley, Shameca McClary, Betty Council, Mary Frederick, Joyce Dickerson, Terry Kennerly, Shakeia Lawhorn, Brains & Beauty Book Club, Janaeda Knicole, Wilgena B. McGee, Deborah Lockard, Victoria Hickson, Cynthia Jones, Rugenar Sowers & BooksAMillion Stores.

Table of Contents

CHAPTER 1 9
CHAPTER 2 14
CHAPTER 3 33
CHAPTER 4 38
CHAPTER 5 55
CHAPTER 6 65
CHAPTER 7 72
CHAPTER 8 78
CHAPTER 9 93
CHAPTER 10 98
CHAPTER 11 106
CHAPTER 12 127
CHAPTER 13 137
CHAPTER 14 144
CHAPTER 15 147
CHAPTER 16 160
CHAPTER 17 173
CHAPTER 18 191
CHAPTER 19 210
CHAPTER 20 216
CHAPTER 21 224

CHAPTER 1

Do you believe in love at first sight?
Well, Jordan Banks didn't either until the
day she met Dr. Tobin Douglas.

* * *

Jordan Banks thought she was the
happiest girl on the planet until the day her
happiness was torpedoed to hell by the man
she'd loved more than three years. Jordan
had spent a wonderful night of passionate
lovemaking with Frank, her beau, before
that fateful morning she left home excited,
extremely happy on her way to work as a
Math teacher at the local high school, while
Frank had crawled out of her warm bed, got
dressed, went off and married someone else.
The shock and hurt from his betrayal left her
in a state of misery and pain, so much so
that she made a rash and unexpected
decision to go to Montego Bay, Jamaica.
She made reservations for one week, packed

a bag and along with her broken heart and an empty wallet, she boarded a plane for a getaway she knew she couldn't afford. All she wanted was to try and leave behind the pain that had gripped her heart unmercifully.

After arriving in Jamaica and checking into the hotel, Jordan spent much of her time in her room. She ate whatever meals she was able to force down, she read magazines and occasionally, she stared out the window at the gorgeous beaches.

On the very last day of her stay on the island, Jordan went to the beach where she met Dr. Tobin Douglas, an oncologist who resided in Atlanta. They spent the day learning as much about each other that one day would allow and by the end of the night, she and Toby had fallen in love, only to have her board a plane the next day to return to Georgia, leaving him there on the island.

Forty-five minutes was just enough time for Jordan to make her way from the Atlanta International Airport to catch her connecting flight to Augusta. Bursting with excitement, her beautiful face lit u, smiling because of thoughts of Toby floating around inside her head. Jordan found her seat, settled in and pulled a magazine from the rack in front of her and began leafing through the pages.

After a while and unable to concentrate, she returned the magazine to its holder and gazed out to see white clouds billowing passed the window.

Over the next twenty-four hours after meeting , she thought of how Toby wined, dined and pampered her, giving her feelings she could never have imagined and since that time, she'd not been able to get him out of her mind.

It wasn't long before a flight attendant pushed a cart down the aisle with drinks and snacks. Jordan made her selection but before she could finish her treats, the plane had landed.

She got out of her seat. She picked up her purse, pulled a small bag from the overhead compartment, and she exited the plane. After picking up her car from the extended parking section at the airport she drove to her house.

It was almost dark when she pulled into her garage. Jordan dropped her bag on the floor in the foyer and walked across the street to her neighbor's house. The door opened and Jordan was warmly greeted by a woman in her early seventies who wore an apron over a blouse and pants and a huge smile on her pretty brown face.

"Well, hello there, Miss Jamaica," the elderly woman said. They embraced.

"Hey Mrs. Irene," Jordan replied, as they released each other.

"Come on in and tell me about your trip. You want something to drink?"

"What you got?" Jordan asked, following Mrs. Irene into her kitchen. "Something sure smells good up in here.

"The House Special from Mr. Wong's Kitchen has always been my go-to place when I've had a long day away from home and don't have time to cook. I know you cooked a lot of food for me before you left and I definitely will get to it, but I had a taste for Mr. Wong's today . You're welcome to some," Mrs. Irene offered, going over to the refrigerator.

"No, thanks." Jordan sat at the table. "How was your day?"

"I read to the kids at the hospital, then I spent time at the Council Street Nursing Home and talked with the folk over there. I wore that crème colored suit you made for me and girl, I got so many compliments." Mrs. Irene smiled, her eyes sparkling and bright as she pulled a pitcher of lemonade from the refrigerator that she placed with ice and two glasses on the table.

"You had a busy day. I hope you aren't doing too much."

"No! It keeps me young and frisky." Chuckling, Mrs. Irene filled both glasses and handed one to Jordan before she took a seat across from her.

Jordan was still chuckling when she said, "I know they appreciate you."

Mrs. Irene took a sip from her glass and set the glass back down on the table. "Now," she said, resting her arms on the table, "tell me all about Montego Bay."

CHAPTER 2

Jordan filled Mrs. Irene in on the details of her trip. Sharing the time she spent with Toby, each syllable of the story caused her eyes to swim while her chest rose and fell with excitement. "And, that was how I spent my time in Jamaica," she concluded, took a deep breath and said, "So you see, my trip turned out to be, well, not so bad."

Mrs. Irene sighed happily with both hands pressed against her chest. "What happened that last day definitely has my heart doing flip flops," she chuckled. "You should have brought Dr. Tobin Douglas back here with you."

I wish I could have, Jordan thought.

Then, Mrs. Irene's facial expression changed. She asked, "So, what's going on with that Frank?"

Jordan sighed deeply. "I haven't spoken with him so there is nothing to tell."

"I always knew there was something I didn't trust about that boy."

"You did?!"

"Sure did."

"Why didn't you say something?" Jordan asked, lacing her fingers together on the table. "He seemed responsible enough; he owns a business, works hard, spent quality time with me. What did I miss? How did I miss so much? And, what does that say about me?"

"He fooled everybody, baby."

"He didn't fool you," Jordan said sadly. "I loved him, Mrs. Irene. He made me feel so much." Her eyes watered over when she said, "Why didn't I see this coming?"

"Love!" Mrs. Irene reached across the table and placed her hands atop Jordan's. "That's what it was. Love makes people do crazy things. Jordan, I've always known you to be a woman who was fearless, full of life, vibrant. You were always bold in your thoughts, your delivery. Everything! Only thing is that you'd never been in love before you got involved with that Frank character. Sometimes women in love lose themselves in the men they fall in love with. You're such a romantic, and if you have a weakness, I'd say it would be that you always looking for the best in people instead of seeing them for who they really are. You give everyone the benefit of the doubt. And, when it comes to love, a woman sees what she wants to see, hear what she wants to hear and thinks what she wants to think, but you're a bright girl, Jordan. I'm sure there were times when you noticed things about Frank that you questioned but you ignored them because you wanted him to be that perfect man when there is no such animal. No one is perfect. You didn't need to convince yourself that things weren't as they seemed just to be with that man."

Jordan looked at Mrs. Irene and nodded in agreement.

"It's alright to be alone until you meet the right man. And you will meet the right man, but you don't have to have a man to validate who you are. Don't ever define yourself by any man. That's not who you are. " She released Jordan's hands.

"Sometimes it gets a little murky. We become so involved or so desperate that we don't always use good judgment." Jordan paused before asking, "Are there always telltale signs?"

"Not always, but more often than not. Sometimes you just got to listen to your instincts. Listen to your gut. Sometimes that tell us all we need to know. Most men will let you know who they are and what they're made of. If they're in it for the game, they want more out of the relationship than they're willing to give, you'll soon know. If they don't show up on holidays, special occasions. If a man isn't conscious enough of your feelings, if he's not willing to make sure that all is good with you," Mrs. Irene stopped short of completing her thought. Then, she added, "If he is willing to reach down and pick you up from the deepest recesses of your life just to make your world better and all he wants in return is your love, then that's your man."

"Does such a man exist?"

"Yeah. There are plenty of good men out there."

Jordan looked thoughtful. Then shaking her head, she said, "I suppose what we believe to be true is true until we don't believe it anymore."

"That's true."

"That man was unbelievable. He was skilled in the art of lying. "

"I believe that." Mrs. Irene agreed, then said, "I'm glad you were able to get away and have a little fun."

Jordan smiled, taking a sip of lemonade.

17

"Have you given any more thought to designing?"

"Yes, but I'm not quite ready to act on that yet. I have some things I'll need to put in place. A business loan would be at the top of that list but since I have the twins' student loans, I'll have to wait a little while for that."

"You know where I stand financially but I'd be glad to help you get started."

"Mrs. Irene, I appreciate your offer more than I can say but I'll get it done, and I promise you, it won't be long."

"Okay, but life is short and you only have one. Sometimes you just gotta act," she said and asked, "Are you sure you don't want something to eat?"

"No, thanks." Jordan finished her lemonade and got up from the table. "I'll probably have a salad later. I ate much more than I should have that last day in Jamaica."

She and Mrs. Irene chuckled.

"Don't worry about that man." Mrs. Irene got up and walked with Jordan to the front door. "You're much better off without him." She looked at Jordan a moment before saying, "You're gonna be fine. You just have to go through this on your own time, at your own pace. Love takes time and you were in love. Give yourself time. If you need to talk later, call me."

"Thank you."

Upon her feet hitting the bottom steps, she heard Mrs. Irene say, "Jordan, don't ever allow anyone to take you away from you."

Jordan smiled and said, "Thank you, Mrs. Irene. Have a good night."

As Jordan crossed the street, she saw Maggie's car parked in front of her house. Jordan was happy to see her friends. They got out of the car, Jordan walked up to them and Jordan, Maggie and Samantha happily embraced each other.

Jordan hadn't spoken to her friends in a week but called on the way from the airport, to let them know she was on her way home.

The three of them entered the house, they took Jordan's bags to her bedroom and placed them on the bed.

"I missed you, girl." Maggie plopped down on the side of the bed as did Samantha.

"You look some kinda good, Missy," Samantha said to Jordan.

"Thanks. So do you two. I missed you two nappy headed gals," Jordan giggled, as she began going through her bags, hanging some things in the closet and tossing others in a pile on the floor to be laundered.

"Love that dress you're wearing." Samantha complimented the lime green, sleeveless fitted dress Jordan was wearing. "You didn't make that one, did you?"

"I did."

"My girls are too young for that dress but they'd still kill for it with their little grown behinds," Samantha chuckled.

"How are Tecali and Shanta?" Jordan inquired about Samantha's daughters.

"They are great." Samantha eyed the dress. "You gotta give that one to me."

"It's yours."

"Are you serious?"

"Girl, the dress is yours. I'll have it cleaned and get it to you this week."

"That was easy. Thanks."

"So how are you doing?" Maggie asked.

"No need to complain." Jordan shrugged her shoulders, taking one empty suitcase and placing it on the shelf in her closet.

Maggie said, "You don't have to put on a brave face for us, Jordan, because we understand what you are going through."

"I don't want you two treating me like I'm a basket case. I'm not some sort of emotional cripple, you know," Jordan smiled reassuringly, brushing a stray piece of hair from her face.

"It's not that. You weren't in a good place when we saw you last." Samantha said.

"I know, but I'm okay. In fact, I'm great. I thought I'd still be in a lot of pain coming back here but fortunately I'm okay."

"I'm surprised because the kind of shit you went through hurts like hell and that kind of pain doesn't go away quickly. I've been there. I know. You guys know that," Maggie said. "When someone breaks your heart, that shit takes time to heal, but I'm glad that you appear to be coping well."

"Seriously, girls, I'm good." Jordan looked from Samantha to Maggie. "Tell me about your trip."

"It was great. We lounged around the pool, sipped margaritas in padded chairs, sipping daiquiris while enjoying the ocean, soaking up some sun, and eyeing those gorgeous island boys." Maggie chuckled.

"And little chocolate mama thought it was in her best interest to put more sun on that skin," Samantha chuckled and Maggie and Jordan joined in.

Maggie always made it a joke about her dark complexion especially since both,

Samantha and Jordan's complexion was very fair.

"Yeah, but I look good," Maggie teased back, and they chuckled some more. "We had a great time, but we were concerned about you, but girl, you look damn good—in fact you look terrific." Then, she changed the subject. "We tried to reach you all week but we couldn't get you. What happened?"

"I went to Montego Bay."

"What?" Maggie's eyes popped wide opened.

"You went to Jamaica?" Samantha asked in pleasant surprise.

"We had no idea you'd be going away. You should've gone with us. We had a blast," Maggie said.

"It was one of those last minute things," Jordan said. "I was moping around, feeling fed up and I figured, what the hell. I made reservations, told the twins of my plans, and after making sure Mrs. Irene was alright, I packed my bags, and I got the heck out of Dodge. When I boarded the plant, I turned off my phone and didn't turn it back on until today when I called you guys."

Maggie said, "I'm glad you were able to get away. It's so gorgeous there, it can make you forget your troubles."

"I was miserable as hell until the very last day," Jordan informed.

"Humph, you look relaxed and gorgeous and got that golden glow going on." Maggie placed a hand on her hip, gave Jordan a side eye saying, "You look happy, like a woman in love. Did something happen in Montego Bay? What aren't you telling us?"

Jordan led Maggie and Samantha to her living room. "Would you two like a glass of wine?" She offered.

"Have you talked with Frank?" Samantha wanted to know.

"Frank?" Jordan asked, a wrinkle in her brow. "No, and I don't want to. I don't want anything else to do with him."

"You know you're going to have to at least talk with him sooner or later. You must have questions, or if anything, you need closure," Samantha said.

"I have all the closure I need."

Maggie shook her head. "You still don't know who he married?"

"No I don't." Jordan was nonchalant with her answer.

"We really should find out who that 'Ho' is and let's do a drive by whip ass session on that bitch. Then hire a couple of thugs to give Frank a good old fashioned beat down,"

Maggie said, laughing only she wasn't joking.

"I'm just so over it," Jordan replied, with a wave of her hand.

"Huh? If I didn't know better, I'd think you went to that island, fell in love and forgot about Frank." Suddenly, it was Samantha's eyes that popped wide open. "You're not in love, are you? Did you meet someone in Montego Bay and fell in love?"

Chuckling, Jordan went to the kitchen. Just as she pulled several glasses from the cabinet, her phone rang. "Mrs. Irene, is everything alright?"

"I'm fine. Just checking on you."

"I'm good. Sam and Maggie are here."

"Okay. You girls enjoy the evening."

Jordan ended the call and returned to the living room, carrying a tray with cheese, crackers, a bowl of cherries, plastic plates, glasses and a bottle of wine. She set the tray on the tale and sat on the couch between her friends. Samantha picked up the bottle of wine and filled their glasses.

"That phone call, it wasn't Frank calling, was it?" Samantha asked, looking at Jordan.

"No. Mrs. Irene was checking on me."

"You didn't answer me before you went off to get the wine and cheese," Samantha returned to their earlier conversation, putting crackers and cheese on her plate.

"What question was that?" Jordan inquired.

"Jordan Dakota Banks, tell me you didn't take your ass off on the heels of a broken heart and fall in love with some stranger on foreign soil," Samantha wailed, biting into a cracker with cheese.

"Seeing how you are now makes me think you did meet someone," Maggie said.

"Did I say that?" Jordan sipping some wine.

"But you're not denying it either." Maggie took a cracker from the plate and popped it into her mouth. "So what's really going on with you?" She probed.

"Yeah, Jordan, girl, tell us." Samantha eyed her.

"I did meet someone." Jordan confessed.

"I knew it. Damn it, I knew it," Maggie exclaimed, slapping a knee. "Who is he? Is he Jamaican? Are you going to see him again?" The questions rolled out of her mouth.

"His name is Tobin Douglas," Jordan shared. "Toby is from Atlanta, he's an oncologist and no, I doubt that I'll ever see or hear from him again."

"Why not?" Maggie wanted to know. "You know what they say."

"What do *they* say?" Jordan asked, although she knew what the answer would be after having heard Maggie repeat it a million times.

"The best way to get over one man is to get right under another," Samantha replied, giving Jordan a sly smile, but it was Maggie who howled with laughter, co-signing.

"How did you two meet?" Maggie asked. "We want details."

"I met Toby my last day on the island," Jordan began, and Samantha and Maggie sat quietly and listened as she shared every detail from when she saw Toby emerging from the ocean to their goodbyes at the airport. "He tried to get me to stay an extra week, but I declined," she added, her eyes began to swim again thinking about the time she and Toby spent together.

"It all sounds so romantic," Samantha said, sighing as she sipped her wine glass.

"And, you didn't even let him put the tip in?" Maggie asked.

"No I didn't. Did you think that I would?"

"I think you should have," Maggie giggled.

"Well no. We didn't go that far."

"Nothing?" Samantha asked.

"We kissed."

"He didn't even go downtown and had a little dessert at mama's kitchen?" Maggie chuckled.

"No," Jordan chuckled also. "I told you we kissed. But one thing for sure, that bad boy knows what to do with a pair of tits."

"Look out now." Maggie giggled out loud, while massaging her own breasts. "So you two did more than just kiss."

Laughing, Jordan waved a hand of dismissal at Maggie.

"Alright now," Samantha laughed and gave Jordan a high five.

"Girl, you shoulda made sure that brother had some condoms, then jump on that thing and ride it like a horse," Maggie chuckled.

"You're crazy," Jordan chuckled.

"Maggie is gangsta," Samantha said.

"Why not? He's not married, is he?" Maggie asked. "

"He said he's not, but you never know what a man will tell you in order to get what he wants." She was reflective a moment, then she said, "I believed him when he said he isn't married. I believed a lot of what he told me." Jordan did wonder whether Toby was telling the truth when he told her he'd fallen in love with her—that it was a case of love at first sight.

"That's the trouble with some of us women. We don't do what we want to do with our own bodies. We do what society expects us to do. Fuck society. If it feels good to me and I'm not hurting anyone, I'm gonna do it." Maggie clicked her teeth. "If he's as nice as you said and he's fine too, I would've stood up on that thing and ground it like a machine. And why not? You'll probably never see him again anyway. So you should have left your mark. Maggie said. "Get him into some of that bondage type shit. Hell, put him in chains, tie his ass up or something."

They all chuckled.

"Are you serious?" Samantha inquired.

"In a heartbeat," Maggie assured her. "Or, he could've tied my ass up and give it to me right, left, sideways upside down."

The three roared with laughter.

"Yeah, and tell him to put on your seat belt because he'd be in for one hell of a ride. Hell, I'm so wet right now just thinking about that shit," Maggie said, and they laughed some more. Jordan said, "Maggie, you've always done things your way, but you're revealing a different side of yourself Tonight, girlfriend."

"This girl has got lots more in her closet, Maggie replied, giggling as she placed a hand against her chest, "than my DKNY and Louis Vuittons."

They giggled.

Samantha said, "That last day you spent in Jamaica must've been one special day."

"It was a day that I'll never forget."

"Well, did he say you would see each other again?" Samantha asked.

"Yes he did, and he appeared serious."

"How do you feel about him? You're not in love with him, are you?" Samantha asked. Jordan ran her finger tip around the rim of her glass.

"I don't think so. Toby is one of the sweetest, most perfect men that I've ever met, and I'm grateful we met at a time when I needed someone so badly, but I'm pretty sure I'm not in love with him. No," she stared off into space, "there was no love connection for me." She got up from the couch. "I picked up a little something for you both from the airport gift shop."

"You did?" said Maggie. "I love gifts."

"What did you get us?" Samantha called after Jordan as she ran off to her bedroom.

"You'll see," Jordan said. "Be right back."

Within minutes Jordan returned with an item draped across her arm and a shopping bag in her hand. She pulled from the shopping bag, two bags of Pistachio nuts and tossed a bag to each of her friends.

"Ooooh, Pistachios," Samantha said, and added, "We picked up a couple of those large sleep-in Tees for you too." Placing her bag of nuts on the coffee table, she then pulled an afghan from the back of the couch and spread it on the floor. They sat on the afghan, facing each other, enjoying their nuts. "I love Pistachios."

"Oh yeah," Maggie said, ripping open her bag, then she asked Jordan, "What you got there?"

Jordan unfolded the item she was holding. "This is a dress Toby surprised me with."

Maggie brushed the residue of the nuts from her hands before taking the dress from Jordan's hand. "Ooh gorgeous, and I know you wore the hell out of it." After giving the dress a once over, she passed it to Samantha to check it out. Maggie said, "I bought a little number when we were on our trip that I'm dying to wear so we have to go out one night soon so I can show it off and turn up." She waved her hands in the air.

"That sounds good," Jordan said and Samantha agreed.

"I love this. It is really sexy," Samantha said, handing the dress to Jordan.

"So you don't think you and Toby will be seeing each other again?" Maggie asked, popping a Pistachio into her mouth.

"I'm really not sure." Jordan took the dress and hung it across the arm of a chair.

"Don't go there, Jordan," Samantha said. "Don't let what happen between you and Frank cause you to have misgivings about other men. Judge each man individually. I don't know this Dr. Tobin Douglas, but I trust your good instincts."

"Where were those good instincts when Frank was leading me down a garden path? I must have thrown those good instincts right out the window." Bitterness seeped out in Jordan's voice.

"Don't be so hard on yourself," Maggie said.

"Frank and I are over, I have accepted that, but it would really be interesting if Toby and I could see each other again. But, if I never hear from him again, not only will I not hold it against him, but I won't ever forget him. That man took me out of such a dark place and made me smile. Hell, the man had me laughing. That was amazing considering where I was when he and I met. He really is someone special. Toby is like no other man that I have ever met. He truly is all that. Handsome, fine, sexy, fire, all of that live in that man's DNA. "

"Wow," Samantha said with glee. "Your own Prince Charming."

"I don't know about *my* Prince Charming but he certainly fits the bill of Prince and Charming."

"I know that's right," Maggie said. "A lot happened in that one day. It really sounds like it was a day in paradise."

"A day in paradise. That's exactly what it was," Jordan eagerly agreed, looking up towards the ceiling with a dreamy look in her beautiful eyes. "If Toby wants to make something happen between us, he'll contact me, and I hope he does—the sooner, the better." Staring off into the distance, she whispered, "A day in paradise." Then, looking from one friend to the other, she tossed a pistachio into her mouth and asked, "More wine ladies?"

CHAPTER 3

At 12:45 that Saturday morning, the sound of thunder could be heard in the distance, followed by a flash of lightning that lit up the sky.

"Sounds like we are in for a stormy night," Jordan said, staring out the window, vividly being reminded of the day she and Toby met in Jamaica and got caught in the rain on the Ferris wheel.   That was the most magical day she'd ever spent with anyone.

"We'd better get going before the rain hits," Samantha said.

"Yeah," Maggie said as she stretched and yawned. "This is it for me, ladies." She and Samantha got up from the floor. "I'm tired and I'm ready for a good night's sleep, that is, after I've pleasured myself sufficiently." Maggie giggled, as she began to clear the coffee table.

"Leave that stuff there, Maggie. I'll take care of that later." Jordan chuckled getting up from the floor. "I can't believe you're still pulling out that old bullet. I thought you were getting it in on the regular."

"I am but not as much as I would like. These men out there are so damn trifling that most of the time, you'd rather not bother. We've lost so many of the good ones, killed off in wars, they're killing each other in the streets or some of them are turning to each other for pleasure. How do you win against that shit? If all this keeps up, I don't know what we women are gonna do for pleasure," Maggie said.

"Don't look at me." Samantha teased.

"Girl, bye." Maggie moaned.

"I'm just saying, if someone isn't coming at me with a stiff one, I can't deal," Samantha said and they all chuckled. "Although my husband spends more time with Uncle Sam than he does with me and the girls, I am and always will be strickly dickly, honey." She chuckled, picking up the afghan filled with Pistachio shells that Jordan reached for.

"I know that's right," Maggie said.

"You're crazy," Jordan said, chuckling. She then took the tray from Maggie's hands and placed the afghan and tray on the coffee table. "Leave that stuff there. I've got it."

"Are you sure?" Maggie said.

"Yeah," Jordan said as she walked Maggie and Samantha to the door.

"What are you doing tomorrow, Jordan?" Samantha asked.

"My cabinets are bare so I'll do a little food shopping, laundry. That's about it."

"Wanna go out for drinks or catch a movie or something?" Maggie suggested.

"I thought you were seeing Gerald this weekend," Jordan replied.

"He'll be working on a brief for some case that's coming up," Maggie replied. "Sometimes I think I should just get myself another man. Any respectable woman wants a good man who holds down a decent job but it makes no sense to have a man who spends the majority of his time working. Mama always says, if your man is less than an hour from you, he should never allow you to miss him. Gerald is less than fifteen minutes away and I miss him all the time."

Jordan said, "I like the way your mama thinks. Then said at the door, "This was fun, you two. Thanks for checking on me."

"Seriously, we have to go out one night and get sloppy drunk. Sam and I will be the designated drivers?" Maggie suggested.

Jordan laughed. "Sounds like a plan."

There was a second boom of thunder, followed again by flashes of lightning, and then, the rain began to fall.

"The rain is here. Let me get you an umbrella," Jordan offered.

"We don't need one." Samantha grabbed Maggie's hand. "Come on, Maggie." They rushed off to the car.

"Get home safely," Jordan called out as they drove away.

It was storming fiercely. Jordan walked over to the window and stared out as the rain pounded the ground and slammed against the window panes while her mind was filled with thoughts of Toby. Where are you, Toby? She wondered. Where are you? Are you thinking of me as I am thinking of you? Tears welled up in her eyes and soon began to slide down her cheeks. She brushed them away with her finger tips.

Jordan turned away from the window. Walking slowly over to the front door, she opened it and walked out onto the porch where she looked up at the dark skies as the rain continued pouring. She lifted her hands in the air as she descended the steps and walked out onto the lawn. With her hands extended towards the sky, she stood there alone—alone in her misery, alone in her pain, while the rain lashed her body, her face, mingling with her unchecked tears.

After a while and completely drenched, Jordan returned inside. After closing the door, on the way to her bathroom, she peeled off the soaked clothing, dropping them in a pile on the floor. She turned on the water in the shower and stepped into the tub, and as the spray of hot water pelted her, she could never remember feeling as lonely or in so much pain. Jordan knew at that very moment that no matter what path her life took, she would certainly never forget Toby. Because, every time it rained, she would think of him and only him.

CHAPTER 4

After drying herself off and slipping into her pajamas, Jordan threw the pistachio shells and plastic plates in the trash and placed the glasses in the sink. She turned off the lights as she made her way to her bedroom and eased into bed. Laying on her back, she stared at the ceiling with thoughts of Toby swirling around inside her head.

Later, turning onto her side, it was then she realized she'd not removed Frank's picture from the night table beside her bed. She picked up the framed picture and staring at it, a sob caught in her throat. It didn't matter how much she denied her feelings, she still cared for Frank—deeply. It also didn't matter how her body still ached with longing for him, she knew she'd have to find a way to move past it. She wished things hadn't changed between her and Frank, but they had, and she knew she'd to reconcile with that as well as a number of facts; she couldn't make Frank love her the way she love him nor could she make him not leave her and go off and marry someone else. Those things were out of her control because he'd done just that, and she had to deal with that reality.

On Monday afternoon, Jordan went through the mail Mrs. Irene had placed on her kitchen table. "Bills, bills, bills," she said, pulling her checkbook from her purse. She wrote checks to cover the bills, walked out to her mailbox and mailed them. Once back inside, Jordan got dressed, she picking up a pile of clothes from her bed and carried them to her car. After starting the car, she popped a CD into the player, and she left her house with the music blasting. She dropped off items at the cleaners, shopped for groceries, and within a couple of hours, she headed home. She was nodding her head and humming to a popular tune coming from the CD player as she approached her house. She was surprised to see Frank's motorcycle parked out front.

Jordan had not seen Frank or spoken to him since the day he left her warm bed after making love to her and married another woman. Her hands began shaking as she gripped the steering wheel. Her heart pounded against her rib cage and she began perspiring profusely. Why is he here? Hadn't he already torn her life apart? What could he possibly have to say to me now? Anger rushed back at full throttle as she turned into her driveway. She glared at the motorcycle and for one brief second, she was tempted to run her car over it, squash it to pieces. Instead, she entered the garage.

Jordan ran the back of her hand across her forehead, removing the perspiration that had formed there. She got out of the car, removed groceries from the trunk and as she put her key in the kitchen door lock and sudden the door flew opened and there stood Frank, smiling at her as though nothing had happened between them.

"Let me help you with those," he said, reaching for the bags she was carrying.

"What are you doing here, Frank?" she asked, angrily, pushing past him, not only because he still had keys to her house and she'd not thought to change her locks, but also because he had the audacity to bring his cocky, no good, lying, married ass into her home without an invitation or her knowledge.

"Damn baby, you look good," he complimented, looking her up and down.

"What do you want, Frank?" she asked, smelling his cologne, the one she liked so much. She slammed the bags down on the table and began putting the groceries away.

"You!" he said simply. "I want you. I came here to get you back."

Without looking in his direction, Jordan continued putting away the groceries. "It is over, Frank! I don't want you in my life or my house. It is done!"

"You're everything to me, Jordan. You're everything I want in a woman. How I got off track, I really don't know. I do know that even broken things can heal. I made a mistake but I'm back."

Jordan stopped what she was doing to glance over at him and asked, "Did I stutter? It's over, Frank! Over!"

Ignoring her response, he asked, "Where you been? I been trying to reach you all week. You look great."

She turned to him again, this time affixing him with a stare. "Why are you here?"

"We need to talk."

"Talk?" she echoed. "What's there to talk about?" She placed her hands on her hips and narrowed her eyes. "That you laid your ass in my bed, screwed me all night, then you got up in the morning and married someone else? Did I get something wrong?"

Jordan's eyes pierced into his like a knife slicing through soft butter. She turned away and resumed putting items into cabinets, the refrigerator, banging doors as she went.

Frank moved around in front of her and facing her, he raised his palms. "Will you please let me talk to you?"

"If you're here to lobby for yourself after blowing my life to hell, have fun with that."

"Jordan...."

"Look," she interrupted, "you have already shown me exactly who you are. I didn't realize you were that kind of man but worse, I don't know how I could've been so fooled by the shit you were unloading, that's the shit that baffles me most."

"Hold up a minute, will you?" He moved closer to her.

"Get out of my way." She brushed past him and tossed the empty grocery bags into the trash.

"Will you please let me explain what happened?"

Jordan turned stone cold eyes on him. "I already know what happened so what else is

there to say? You're sorry? Well, if that's
what you want to say, trust me, that ain't
gonna cut it." After placing the last items
into the freezer, she turned and glared at him
again. "I can't believe you have the
unmitigated gall to bring your deceiving,
sorry ass back here after what you did. I
don't believe it. What do you hope to
accomplish now? Rub my face in it?"

"Why I gotta be sorry?!"

Shaking her head, she turned away,
yanked a glass from the cabinet and after
pulling a bottle of wine from the fridge and
filling her glass, she took a huge gulp.

"Jordan," Frank began softly, "I know
you're angry at me, and I don't blame you. I
got caught up in some silly ass shit. I don't
know how it happened. All I can say is that
I'm not in love with her. I was never in love
with her—never! She had me thinking she
was pregnant and then…" Realizing he'd
said too much, he stopped.

Jordan stared at Frank as if she was
seeing him for the first time. "So you
thought she was pregnant!"

"I made a mistake. I was a damn fool."

"Gee, you think." She took another
healthy sip of wine.

"What I did was stupid, downright crazy."

"Give this man a prize," she sipped her wine again before putting her glass down.

Frank walked up to Jordan and gripped her upper arms. "I'm sorry, baby. Please believe me. I made a mistake."

"What is this? A broken record?"

"What I did was wrong, but I don't want to lose you." He sighed, heavily. "I got into a bad situation but I'm correcting it. I've told her it's over, I moved out, and I'm in the process of having the marriage annulled. I'm gonna fix this, Jordan. I promise you."

Jordan leaned against her countertop and said, "If this is it, you're failing miserably."

"Doesn't what I'm doing mean anything to you?" He said, emphatically.

She stared at him in disbelief. "What do you want from me, a gold star?!"

"No. A second chance. Don't I deserve a second chance? I love you. I never stopped loving you, and I'm here now, asking for your forgiveness."

"Second chance. Ha. Do you think I could ever trust you again? You destroyed all of that." She looked into his dark, bedroom eyes, at the strong bone structure of his cheeks and jaw that'd always made her stomach does flip-flops and said without difficulty, "I am done. I want nothing more to do with you. Ever!"

"I don't expect it to happen overnight but I promise I will work hard to earn your trust again—and your love." He looked deeply into her eyes. "I love you, and I miss you like crazy. I can't lose you, baby! I can't!" He paused a moment before saying, "I'm sorry about how things went down. I'm hoping that with time, you will remember what we had, what we meant to each other. I hope then that we can start over, rebuild."

"Rebuild?! She screamed. "There's nothing left to rebuild. It is over and done with!"

"You remember when we went to Florida all the fun we had and promised we'd go back. You remember how great that was?"

Of course, she remembered that trip. It was the best trip she'd ever had, but if he thought trying to refresh her memory of one nice time they had and assume it would make this bad situation go away, he was sadly mistaken. "There is no question that we had some nice times together but let me remind you that everything about our relationship wasn't all good either," she said, remembering when she and Frank were dating while he was in the Army, there were times when he'd come home and return to the base without seeing her. Because she loved him so much, there were things she overlooked. Yes, there were good times they shared, but there were also painful times that she would never forget.

"I know that. No relationship is perfect but you've gotta admit, what we had was good and strong and all I'm saying is that if we can put the bad aside and concentrate on the good, I know we could make this work."

Even angrier now, she gave him her full attention. "You haven't been listening to me. What is it about, *I'm done*, don't you get? Look, I'm a grown ass woman, I make up my own mind about what I'm gonna do with my life, and I no longer see you in it. So, I'm gonna repeat this once more, go home to your wife, Frank, and make your marriage work because there is nothing you can say or do to make me change my mind about you. There is nothing here for you. So go!" She raised both hands and with a scowl on her face, she added, "Just go."

"Please don't look at me like that, like I disgust you or that you hate me."

"Take it however you want. I really don't care."

"Don't you think you're overreacting?"

"Overreacting? Are you really saying that to me?" Her eyes shone with anger as she jerked her finger toward the wine bottle on the table, "If I were, I would have hit you up side your head with that wine bottle."

"See, you do care," he wailed, enthusiastically. "If you didn't care, you wouldn't even think about going gansta on my ass." They stood a moment, staring at each other with no words being spoken. Then, Frank asked, "Have you forgotten me so quickly? You don't love me no more? You're the only woman that I want, the only one that I need. You know that, don't you?"

She looked at Frank, scorn on her face. "How could you do this to me?" she asked harshly. "I loved you, Frank. I thought I was everything you wanted, and I would've done anything for you, but that wasn't enough. You took the light out of my eyes and the joy out of my heart. You didn't care about me. You threw it all away. You get that, don't you?!"

"Yeah, but Jordan, you're the best thing that's ever happened to me and the thought of not having you in my life drives me crazy. I've got to get you back."

"Keep telling yourself that," Jordan said, glaring at him with cold, distrustful eyes.

"You couldn't have forgotten all the love we shared in one week. I'm sorry. It just doesn't work that way. What we had was special. I know that and so do you.."

"I don't know what kind of fool you think that I am." She threw up her hands in disgust. "Look, I'm not doing this."

It took all the strength she had inside to keep from beating his ass. There was no denying she still had feelings for Frank, but after meeting Toby, she thought some of her anger had subsided. Not true. Now, she felt her anger again, taking on a life of its own, bubbling up inside, again. She turned to walk away from him but turned back and said, "I can't believe you would expect me to take your ass back after you pulled a fucking 180 on me."

"Where did you learn to talk like that? You never talked like that." He chuckled. "But, I've gotta say, it is sexy as hell seeing you mad and standing up for yourself like that. It turns me on."

"Who are you? I don't even know who you are. You knew what you were going to do all along but you didn't have the decency to tell me, yet you come here now begging me to take you back." Jordan was now screaming at the top of her lungs, and unable to hold back her tears any longer. She began to cry. "Give me back my keys, get your tired ass out of my house and don't come back."

Frank rushed up to Jordan, wrapped his arms around her and held her closely, tightly, restricting her movement.

"All that fire, all that passion. I love the hell out of that. That really turns me on."

Jordan struggled to free herself from his grip. "Why did you do this to me when you knew how I felt about you? Why did you hurt me like that?" She said remembering the last morning they spent together when she asked him to not leave her. At the time, she had no idea why she'd said that but she must have had some instinct about him, one she didn't want to acknowledge even to herself.

"I fucked up. I thought Claudia was pregnant and I didn't want my child to be born out of wedlock the way that I was. I was just trying to do the right thing. For the child. I just went about it the wrong way. Anyway, the marriage is done."

"I don't care. Just get your hands off of me," she screamed, still trying to break free of his grip, but Frank continued to hold her.

"Shhhhhh," he said. "Don't cry. I love you, Jordan, and I'm sorry. Please don't cry. I'm so sorry." He lowered his head and nuzzled his face against her neck. Then, he raised his head and his mouth came down hard, covering hers. Jordan managed to tear her mouth from his, she freed an arm and slapped him hard across his face. Still Frank held her in his grip. As she sobbed and was unable to free herself, she went limp in his arms and cried for what seemed like a very long time.

After she'd cried out all her renewed misery, all her fresh pain, she tried to untangle herself. It took a moment for Frank to loosen his grip on her and looked down into her face. Completely exhausted now and in slow motion, Jordan moved away from him, brushing tears from her face."

"Do something for me?" He asked.

She moved further away from him, putting more distance between them and spat out, "You keep invading my personal space and I am so sick of it."

"Please?"

She turned an infuriating stare at him and before she could stop herself, with her free hand, she slapped him hard across the face with an open palm. He gasped with shock that matched her own. She had no intention of striking him but now that she had, hell, it felt good. As a matter of fact, it felt great!

"Wow," he said, smiling and rubbing his sore cheek. "That was quite a hit."

"What do you want?"

He relaxed his hand and asked, "Did I tell you I have a little surprise for you?"

"You're insane or full of yourself more than you realize."

"Come on, Jordan. Humor me. Come with me." He reached for her hand. "Come."

Angrily, she snatched her hand away. "Let's just get this over with."

Jordan didn't miss the devilish gleam that fired Frank's dark eyes as she followed him down the hall and watched as he opened the door to *her* living room. Not his living room! Her living room! And immediately, the aroma of Chinese food hit her in the face. She couldn't believe the nerve of him as a deeper level of anger swept over her.

On the coffee table, Frank had candles lit, wine chilling and takeout of their favorite Chinese food were on display on the table.

She couldn't count the times they sat at that coffee table, ate Chinese food and drank wine before ending their evening in bed, making love, passionately through the night.

Interrupting her thoughts, Frank said, "It took so long to convince you to come in here that my candles nearly burned out."

Disgusted at Frank's continuous weak attempts to smooth things over with her, she turned a cold dark eye on him. "What is this, Frank? What are you doing?"

He walked over to the couch, picked up two pillows and tossed them on the floor at either end of the coffee table. "Please....sit."

Jordan was incredulous. She had about as much of his antics as she could stand. She stomped around the coffee table. "I don't believe this." She picked up a container of food and hurled it at Frank. Then another. And another, spilling food all over him, the table and the floor. "I told you to get your ass out of my house," she yelled, continuing to toss items, knives, forks, napkins, food and wine at Frank. "I want you out of here! NOW!" She screamed.

"Alright, alright," Frank said, taken aback by Jordan's strong refusal of his gesture. He brushed food from his face, his clothes and hands, regretting he didn't get the response he hope for. "I'll leave but I know you, Jordan, and I know you still love me. You can't just sweep feelings like what we shared under a rug. It takes time for feelings like that to go away—a lotta time."

Jordan was so overwhelmed and weak with raw emotions that she couldn't speak. She could only point a finger towards the door. She thought she'd spend the rest of her life with Frank. There was no reason to believe otherwise. At least that was what she thought. She loved him more than she thought was possible to love another human being and had expected him to be her future. He'd made her feel safe, wanted, protected and loved. She wanted to have his children and grow old with him. But all that had changed now.

"I'm still the man you were in love with," he said, "I'm here, and I'm all in and willing to do whatever it takes. I'm still that Frank! Your Frank, Jordan!"

"If you felt that way, you wouldn't have done what you did and we wouldn't be having this conversation. So," she scowled. "I don't care about the status of your situation; married—not married, I don't give a damn. Fir the last time, get the hell out of my house and leave my keys," Jordan shouted, then added, looking directly into his eyes, "Let me tell you something. I'm not that same Jordan you screwed and left a week ago and if you keep testing me, I'm go from that pet goldfish to a very aggressive, mother fucking shark. You got that?"

"Jordan."

She interrupted him. She wanted her situation with Frank over. Now! "Since nothing I've said appears to be sinking in, try this, FUCK YOU!" she screamed. "How about that? Does that work better for ya?" She shook her head in disgust more with herself then Frank. "I realize something about myself, finally. I deserve much better than you. Now leave or I'm calling the police," she finished in a calmer voice.

His cell phone rang. He pulled it out of his pocket and after checking the number, he returning it to his pocket. He then pulled a ring of keys from another pocket. "Okay, if that's what you want," he said, putting the keys on the coffee table, and not taking his eyes off her until he turned and walked out. Upon hearing the door close behind Frank, she dropped down on the couch and with her head in her hands, she sobbed.

CHAPTER 5

That morning, Jordan opened her eyes and saw eight o'clock reflecting on the digital clock on her night table. She got out of bed and remembering what she had to face caused her to groan out loud. Cleaning up that Chinese food she threw at Frank last night that not only landed on him, but the furniture, the walls, the living room floor, would be a chore. She sighed, got up from the bed and dressed quickly before going into the kitchen to make breakfast.

At 9:15, she rang Mrs. Irene's doorbell, carrying a tray with two plates of food and coffee for the two of them.

Mrs. Irene opened the door, wearing a robe and slippers. "Good morning," she greeted Jordan with a bright smile.

"How are you doing," Jordan said as she entered the house and followed Mrs. Irene into the kitchen. After placing the food and coffee on the table and after the blessing, they sat and began to eat.

"You don't have to bring me food every day." Mrs. Irene put eggs into her mouth."

"Of course I'm gonna bring you breakfast." Jordan got up from the table and returned with several paper napkins that she put on the table and returned to her seat.

"You take such good care of me. You must have more important things to do on your summer break than waiting on me."

"I love you and I enjoy having breakfast with you. You always take good care of the twins and me. Especially when we were little. You were always there and you still are. I don't know what we would've done without you. This is a very small gesture to let you know that we appreciate you."

"Well, I appreciate you." Mrs. Irene sipped from her cup. "I saw that bike parked over at your house yesterday."

"Yeah." Jordan took a bite of bacon.

"What did he have to say for himself?"

"He tried to tell me he made a mistake, he was going to make it right between us and that I should give him a second chance. I told him I wasn't interested and to get out."

"Is that how you really feel?"

"I'm disappointed but I'll get over it." Jordan bit off another piece of bacon, then she forked more food into her mouth.

Mrs. Irene sipped more coffee and held the cup in her hand. "That boy doesn't have a bit of character. He shows you just who he is by his actions. And when someone puts it out there, what are you going to do? You ain't got no choice but to believe what they are showing you, because that's exactly who they are."

"You're never gonna believe what I did, Mrs. Irene."

"What did you do?"

"Lover boy didn't leave as neat and clean as when he arrived."

"What happened?" Mrs. Irene looked at Jordan with raised eyebrows.

When Jordan shared what she'd done to Frank, Mrs. Irene's eyes popped opened and her mouth formed a perfect circle. Then, they burst into laughter.

Still laughing, Mrs. Irene said, "Please tell me you're joking."

"I'm not joking," Jordan laughed.

"You threw food on the man?"

"I sure did."

"Chinese food?"

"Yes Ma'am."

"As much as you and I love Chinese food you couldn't have found something else to throw at his ass."

Jordan laughed out loud. She'd never heard Mrs. Irene swear before and it was funny hearing it that first time.

"I hope some of those boxes hit him right up side that old big head of his," Mrs. Irene said, and they laughed some more.

"I just threw the boxes at him, hoping they all hit their intended target. When he left, he was in need of a shower and he would have a cleaning bill as well. You know he wears nice clothes. But, for me, unfortunately, my living room also needs a good cleaning."

They laughed again.

When the laughter stopped, Mrs. Irene looked at Jordan with a serious expression on her face. "You're going to be just fine. There's a good man out there for you. You're drop dead gorgeous, you're as smart as they come and you have a tremendous heart. You could have any man you want. You just got to allow that little girl inside you come out and be who she is. Don't be so serious all the time. Play a little. Have fun." Mrs. Irene smiled, a little twinkle in her warm brown eyes.

Later, Jordan cleared the table and as she washed the dishes, they talked and around eleven, she returned to her house. She grabbed a pail with water, some cleaning products, and she went into the living room and stared at the mess. Then, she decided she'd better get started because the room wasn't gonna clean itself and she began cleaning up the mess that she made.

Jordan cleaned everything in the room only stopping once to have a glass of water and by seven o'clock that evening, the house was completely clean, Jordan showered, changed into her night gown and was running a towel through her wet hair, contemplating what she'd have for dinner when her doorbell rang. She dropped the towel on the bed, slipped into a robe and went to answer the door.

Mrs. Irene breezed into the house with a tray in her hands. "I brought you dinner."

"I was just wondering what I was gonna eat." She took the tray from Mrs. Irene's hands. "Spaghetti. You know I love your spaghetti. Come on in and let's eat."

Mrs. Irene followed Jordan into the kitchen and before long, they were sitting across from each other enjoying a garden salad, followed by spaghetti and meatballs, corn on the cob, rolls and ice tea.

"Mrs. Irene, you know how I feel about becoming a designer."

"Ever since you were a little girl."

"When I was in Jamaica, I met a couple who gave me some information that looked promising. I think I might give them a call."

"Sounds good. When you want something bad enough, you'll find a way to make it happen. Don't give up on your dreams. If it works out for others, it'll work out for you."

"You believe I can do this, don't you?!"

"You bet your life I do and you really don't have anything to hold you back. The twins have gotten their education and are making a life for themselves. It's time you do the same. Besides, I've seen your designs, have worn some of them, and I'd put your work right up there with the top designers. Honey, their work ain't no better than yours. As a matter of fact, I think your designs are better than most." Mrs. Irene chuckled. "You got to give it a try. You know what they say."

"No, Mrs. Irene, what do they say?"

"You can't make an omelet without first breaking a few eggs."

Jordan and Mrs. Irene stared at each other a moment before they burst into laughter. "You are too much."

"But it's true. You got to break that egg to get the process started."

"You say those things because you love me, but I appreciate it anyway. Thank you!"

"Sure I love you and the twins, Jordan, but what I say to you are what I know in my heart to be true."

It was after 9 o'clock that night when Jordan walked Mrs. Irene home. When Jordan returned to her house, she went into the kitchen, poured herself a glass of wine that she took to her bedroom as her cell phone rang. "Hey, Steffie," she answered.

"How was Jamaica?" Steffie asked.

"It was incredible. You should go one day."

"I might just do that."

"I bought you and Stevie a little something."

"Sis, you really don't have to keep buying us stuff. We aren't kids anymore, and we've got jobs."

"So how is your new place coming along and what would you like as a housewarming gift? And, don't go too expensive on me. You know my finances," Jordan chuckled. After graduating college and working a year, Steffie and Stevie bought a house together. Jordan gave them eighteen months to get out of school before requiring them to begin repayment of their student loans. Since they would begin that process in six months, Jordan was surprised they'd embarked on a purchase so costly so soon. "When am I gonna see you and your brother new place?"

"That's why I'm calling. Stevie and I are having a little get together next Friday, and we want you to come."

"That's over on Jefferson, right?"

"That's right. At 9 o'clock."

"That's one of those pricey neighborhoods, isn't it?"

"We have jobs, Jordan."

"What do I need to bring?"

"Just your appetite and a pleasant, happy attitude." After a moment, she said, "You haven't said anymore about Frank." Jordan had shared with the twins her breakup with Frank, but she was moving pass that and didn't want to talk about him anymore. "I know how you felt about him, so how are you dealing with the fall out?"

Jordan let out a silent breath. In all honesty, she wasn't dealing with the situation very well, especially with Frank popping in unexpectedly. Her and Frank's relationship covered a three-year period, and you don't get over losing someone you thought was important in your life so easily.

"Frank isn't the man I thought he was and that's about all I can say." She shrugged her shoulders. "It is what it is."

"He wasn't good enough for you anyway," Steffie said, harshly. "You're still the best thing that's ever happen to him and the best damn chick that I know. Jordan, you are an awesome person, you constantly inspire others, and you always try to make other's lives better. Can't get much better than that. Well, I gotta run. Lots of calls to make. Nine o'clock next Friday, okay?"

"Got it."

"Love you."

"Love you more."

They ended the call. Jordan placed the phone back on the table, picked up her glass of wine and sipped from it. Suddenly, she felt sad. It was odd that her thoughts didn't go to Frank. They went to Toby, the day they met, the time they spent together. She remembered everything about Toby; his face, his smile, his eyes, his body, and the kisses they shared. Jordan had never been kissed by anyone the way Toby had kissed her. The memory of those kisses was seared in her brain and caused her body to catch fire. She tried shutting Toby out of her mind but she had to admit, it wasn't working.

Jordan had said goodbye to Frank and Toby and although for entirely different reasons, she decided that her life would've been so much better without the likes of Frank Benjamin and his lying ass. But Toby! He was a different story. Only he was so far out of her life now. It was almost as though they'd never met except for the twinge she felt in her heart every time she thought of him and that was often. Toby said he'd be in touch with her but there was no reason to think she'd ever hear from him again. What she did know for sure was that she'd never be able to get him out of her mind or her heart. Plain and simple.

CHAPTER 6

Jordan arrived at Stevie and Steffie's new home at eight o'clock. She knew the neighborhood was upscale but this was even beyond her expectations. When the front door opened, Steffie greeted her. Jordan was carrying two sweet potato pies that she baked that morning for the occasion.

The sisters embraced.

"Wow!" Jordan exclaimed, looking around. "This is really nice."

"Thank you. We do try." Steffie took the pies from Jordan's hands, and she danced off towards the dessert table, with Jordan following her. They unwrapped the pies and placed them on the table. "Have you heard from your doctor friend?"

"No! But I didn't tell you when you called the other day that Frank came by?"

"You lying."

"Can you believe it?"

"What did that lying ass have to say for himself?"

"He was an ass but that's a conversation for another time."

"Men. Screw 'em.   But, look, I've got someone I want you to meet anyway."

"Stephanie Breslyn Ikia Banks, don't you mess with me," Jordan warned. "I'm fresh out of one relationship and I'm definitely not in a hurry to get into another."

"Girl, stop being an old lady and live a little. You're too hot not to."

Before long the house was crowded. Steffie and Stevie introduced Jordan to their friends, then she walked with Steffie across the room to a man who appeared to be alone, and she made the introduction. "Jordan, this is Walt, a really good friend of mine. Walt, this is my sister, Jordan." The two shook hands and extended pleasantries. "I'm leaving you in very capable hands. Have fun. I'm about to mingle." With that, she left Jordan and Walt to entertain each other.

Jordan and Walt engaged in conversation and they even danced a little. She knew what her siblings were trying to do and she appreciated it, but after dinner, Jordan feigned exhaustion, she begged off and was leaving when Stevie caught her hand and walked her to the door.

"You sure you are ready to leave. The guys in here have been checking you out all night but it looked like Walt didn't intend on giving anyone else a chance."

"I don't know what I'm gonna do with you and that sister of yours."

"I also saw the looks you were giving Monkey and me all evening. What's on your mind?"

"Your home is really lovely, Stevie."

His eyes swept the room then he turned back to his sister. "Thank you."

"Enjoy your party. We'll talk soon." With that, Jordan left.

The following day, Jordan answered the doorbell and she wasn't surprised to see her brother standing there. Where's your key?"

"I left it home."

"Come on in." Jordan stood back and allowed her brother to enter. "We've got some things to talk about."

"That's why I'm here. I want to get it over with so I can breathe again," he chuckled, following Jordan to the couch.

She sat down and patted the couch for him to sit. "I just want to know how in the hell can you and Steffie afford a place like that? In a few more months I'll be turning over your student loans to you. How are you and Steffie gonna manage with that expensive house, plus your other financial obligations," Jordan said, with concern.

"We're managing, Jordan. You don't have to worry about us."

"But I do worry. I wish you two would pace yourself. I'm afraid you guys are biting off more than you can chew. You don't have to have everything all at once. There'll be plenty of time to get the things you want. Just don't rush it."

"Monkey is handling the largest portion of the mortgage but everything else, we're going fifty/fifty."

"I have an idea what Steffie is bringing home from her nursing position, and I know she's holding down some part time job. I also know that you're making decent money from your Tech job, but that house. It's got to be at least half a million. What kind of part time work is Steffie doing anyway?"

"You're gonna have to ask her that."

"I know you know and if she's gonna tell anyone, it's gonna be you. There are no secrets between you and your sister." Then, she turned and looked Stevie in his eyes. "What is this part time job that she has?"

"I don't know."

"Stevie."

"I really don't know. All she's told me is that she works in the evening and it pays well. That's all I know."

"Stevie, you do know."

"I'm telling you that I don't."

"I know one thing. This job had better be on the up and up."

"Monkey doesn't really talk to me about her work. You know growing up, Monkey always wanted more than we could afford. She was never satisfied with ordinary stuff. She always tried to make sure she got what she wanted. And, the few times when she couldn't, that girl was hard as hell to get along with," Steven laughed and Jordan smiled, shaking her head, remembering those days. "Now that we have jobs, she's determined to have what we couldn't afford back then." Stevie paused a moment, then said, "Don't worry about us, Jordan. We're fine. Monkey tells me what she needs from me each month, I give it to her and we're straight."

She gave her brother a dark look. "That's what scares the hell out of me. She wants it all and she wants it now."

"It's all good. Monkey and I are fine."

She looked at Stevie. "If you say so, but you'd better not let her hear you call her Monkey."

"I won't tell if you don't."

Steven and Jordan burst into laughter.

Then Jordan changed the subject. "Tell me about that little trip you and your sister went on. I was a bit concerned about you, not too much about Steffie because she's pretty level headed about traveling and that sort of thing."

"But, I'm the bad boy, right?"

"Yes you are, so tell me, did you become the stud of the week?"

Stevie laughed, heartily. "That depends on what you mean about being a stud. If you want to know if I had sex while on vacation, the answer is yes—lots of it."

"Stevie," Jordan said, giving him a look.

"I was careful."

"You used protection every time?"

"Down girl," he gestured with his hands. "Did you?"

"Come on, Sis. Can we not do this?"

"I'm serious."

This time, Stevie gave Jordan a look. "What am I, twelve?"

"No, you're not, but it only takes one slip up to screw up. Sometime young people go off on these fun vacations, lose their heads and, well, they ruin their lives which can happen by one mistake, you know. There's so much crap going on out there."

"I wish you would give me credit for having some sense. Besides, you've spent too much time worrying about me and Monkey. We're not kids anymore. We exercise good judgment." Stevie glanced at his sister who gave him another look. "Well, most of the time. Anyway, rest assured, I was careful with the white girls, the black girls, the Asian girls and all the other girls."

Jordan picked up a pillow and hit her brother with it.

"I'm just kidding."

"I hope so."

"I'm good. So, enough of that. Now, let's talk about you."

She frowned. "What about me?"

He knew Jordan didn't want to talk about Frank and decided not to pressure her. "That Frank is just a loser anyway. Good riddance to him."

"Yeah. Good riddance to him."

CHAPTER 7

Jordan sat at the kitchen table and dialed the number to Michael and TaNisha Turner's Design House in Atlanta. She'd already called twice, left a message each time and had not gotten a returned call. No answer. She left another message and hung up. She got up from the table, pulled a pitcher of lemonade from the refrigerator and poured herself a glass. She picked up her sketch pad from the kitchen table and went into the living room. She placed all the sketches on the table, reviewed them and adding touches to improve them.

Late afternoon, Jordan got dressed and went to a fabric store. After selecting fabrics and other items, she paid the store clerk and returned home. She dropped her purchases on her bed. She kicked off her shoes, removed her clothes and stepped into the shower. She lathered her body with her favorite bath gel as the hot water rained down on her when suddenly, the shower curtain flew open and Toby stepped in. Immediately, his mouth ran over her face, her neck, her shoulder, before seeking out her mouth. She parted her lips and her tongue shot into his mouth.

As the kiss intensified, Jordan's hand moved over his body. Then, her hands went down, cupped him high up between his thighs and she stroked him there. He moaned, satisfied that she wanted him as much as he wanted her. Their tongues sparred, his hands caressed her body and her stroking him intensified. She gave a moan of pleasure when his hands touched her breast, then moved down her body. His fingers located her intimate spot and teased her at the entry to her cavity. He slid one finger into her, then two, moving in and out. Her flesh gripped him and she gyrated against his hand, causing him to catch fire, and he brought her with him.

Toby tore his mouth from hers and moved down to her breasts where he helped himself to a healthy mouthful. She closed her eyes and moaned from the intense pleasure he invoked in her. When neither could stand anymore, he carried her dripping wet body from the tub to her bedroom where they fell together on her bed. His eyes explored her body from head to toe while her eyes took in all he possessed. She couldn't get enough of looking at him and didn't pull her eyes from his massive, hardened member until he climbed atop her, slammed into her and continued plunging into her canal fiercely. She raised her hips and thrust her body against his, causing his mind to border on insanity. With her legs wrapped around his waist, he rose up on his palms and slammed into her unrelentingly, giving her all of him, pleasing her beyond anything she could've ever imagined, with her responding in kind.

When she opened her eyes, the bright sunlight streaming through the bedroom window brought her back to reality. Her body was covered in perspiration, her nightgown, soaked and clinging to her. She turned and stared at the empty space beside her in bed. Toby! It had appeared so real, that he was there with her, making love to her. Only it wasn't real. Toby was not there. It was all a dream. Only she wished that dream was a reality.

Jordan swallowed the lump that had formed in her throat. The very thought of Toby had caused a tightness to form deep inside her stomach. Since Toby had decided to ignore her, she tried to deny her feelings for him, put him out of her mind, but it hadn't happened. The more she tried to forget him, the more she thought about him. Toby was special. There was something about him that set him apart from any other man she'd known. As she sat alone in bed, she wondered whether she'd ever get Toby out of her head and out of her heart.

Jordan threw back the covers, climbed out of bed, pulling the damp covers with her that she carried to the washing machine and set the dial to wash. She'd had several of those so called wet dreams before but what she experienced that morning was the mother lode of wet dreams.

Jordan made breakfast for herself and Mrs. Irene. Later, she went into Steffie's old room that she'd converted into a sewing room, she began going through fabrics for three outfits that she laid out on the table when her phone rang. She checked the caller ID. She'd talk with anyone, even a telemarketer, only she wouldn't talk to Frank. She didn't recognize the number.

"Hello," she answered, poised to hang up depending on who was on the other end.

"Jordan Banks?!" the caller asked.

"Yes."

"Miss Banks, this is TaNisha Turner."

"Hello Mrs. Turner," Jordan responded, excitedly.

"Miss Banks, I apologize for not getting back sooner but what can I do for you?"

Jordan explained her interest in connecting with a design house and that she'd be happy to meet with her and show her designs. "And, if we can make that happen, the sooner the better."

"Yes. Trish spoke very highly of you. She indicated you might be calling, but I'm sorry to say that Michael and I recently closed the business and have sold the space. Trish just learned of it when she called. He and I are no longer together and are in the process of getting a divorce. I wish I could help but as you can see, it's not the best time."

"I understand, Mrs. Turner and may I express how sorry I am about your marriage and your business." They ended the call. Jordan blew out a long breath. She was very regretful about the dissolution of the Turner's marriage and that the business venture didn't materialize as she'd hoped, but that wouldn't stop her. She was going to pursue her dream, she'd make it happen.

She'd never know if she didn't try. It was time to break that egg.

CHAPTER 8

The weeks dragged on interminably.
Frank had called a number of times and left
messages, but Jordan didn't respond. But
she hadn't heard from Toby. After spending
most of her time creating designs, she
decided to take Maggie and Samantha up on
their invitation to go out dancing. At seven
thirty that Friday night, Jordan showered
and after rubbing on some lotion, slipped on
black lace panties and bra and pulled from
her closet, a black mini skirt and a black and
white sheer top that she laid on her bed. She
sat at the bathroom vanity and ran a comb
through her hair and pinned it in a chignon
with tresses cascading around her face. She
lightly put blush on her cheeks, added lip
gloss and sprayed herself with her favorite
White Diamonds Cologne. After slipping
into her outfit, she hooked a pair of silver
earrings into each ear lobes, adding a
matching necklace and bracelet and stuck

her feet into a pair of three-inch black strappy leather heels. She checked herself in the mirror and though she'd lost a little weight, she was satisfied with the way she looked. She grabbed her black leather purse and her keys, and she headed out.

Nine o'clock that evening, Jordan met Maggie and Samantha out front of the theater, they purchased tickets and entered the theater. "You girls are looking good tonight," Jordan complimented.

""You are looking really hot yourself, my friend," Maggie said.

They located seats. While the Coming Attractions were on the screen, Jordan brought them up on Frank's visit and what she did to him and her living room. They squealed with laughter.

After the laughter ceased, Maggie searched through her purse for her phone and responded to a text. Then, she asked, "What did he hope to accomplish?"

"I have no idea," Jordan replied, "but my actions hurt me a hell of a lot more than it did him. It took almost an entire day to clean up that one little room." Maggie and Samantha laughed again. "Chinese food was all over my beautiful cream walls that you guys helped me paint. Food was on the furniture, the floor. The place was a mess."

Samantha was still laughing when she asked, "Was that the only way to get him out of your house?"

"Apparently." Jordan laughed at herself. "But, enough about him. He's no longer a factor."

"That's right," Samantha said. "You've got much bigger fish to fry."

"That's what I'm talking about," Maggie said. "So, have you heard from Toby?"

"No, but I don't think I'm going to."

"I was sure he would've contacted you by now," Samantha said. "It seemed you two had a strong connection."

"That's the impression I got also," Maggie agreed.

"I felt that way also. I felt an attraction for Toby and even people who didn't know us thought we knew each other but for whatever reason, he's chosen not to contact me. Oh well, you win some, you lose some, but you keep it moving," she said, bitterness tearing the joy out of that simple statement.

"Why haven't you contacted him?" Maggie wanted to know.

"I don't have any contact information."

Samantha gave Jordan a look. "How hard can it be to locate Tobin Douglas, oncologist in Atlanta? Give me a break."

"Samantha, you know what this is about," Maggie said. "When someone gets burned, it's not easy to trust again and give your heart unless you are certain the object of your affection is gonna take good care of it."

"That's so elementary," Samantha put in. "If Jordan is interested in the man and she doesn't hear from him, what's to stop her from contacting him? This is the twenty-first century. Girl, call that man. That's what I'd do. What's the big deal?"

The Coming Attractions were finished. The women settled back in their seats and watched The Perfect Boyfriend.

When the movie ended, they exited the theater.

"She really put the screws to him," Maggie chuckled.

"Serve him right," Jordan said and they all chuckled while standing in front of the theater contemplating their next move.

"Let's check out Shadow," Maggie suggested, wiggling her body to her own imaginary music.

"Sounds like a plan," Samantha said.

Jordan said, "Let's do this."

They entered the dimly lit, semi-crowded nightclub and were greeted by fast pace, electric music and high energy dancing. The men looked like tall glasses of water and the women looked extremely thirsty.

Caught up in the music and dancing their way around the club, Maggie said, smiling, "I'm gonna turn this night into my bitch."

They chuckled as they located a small table near the dance floor where they sat and ordered shots. When their drinks arrived, they toasted to making the best of the rest of the summer.

Maggie was the first to notice a group of men staring at them.

"Come and get me, boys," she said, using her hands to bid them on. "Don't be shy."

Three men approached their table, pulled them from their seats and giggling, they hit the floor for a marathon of dancing. After a while, the ladies returned to their table, they ordered fresh drinks. It wasn't long before they returned to the dance floor.

Later, they prepared to leave. Maggie said, "You gals saw the last guy I danced with?"

"Who could miss him?" Jordan asked, "He was hot."

"Yeah, and I'm so wet right now."

"You're kidding," Samantha chimed in.

"Give me your hand. I'll show you," Maggie chuckled.

"Get out of here, you nasty bitch," Samantha chuckled as she slapped Maggie on her back.

On their way out of the club, they ran into others they knew, and they were invited to a birthday party the following month and at two o'clock that morning with their arms linked together, they wobbled to their cars.

Samantha asked, "Are you alright to drive, Jordan?"

"Yeah, I'm a little buzzed but I'm good besides, the coffee shop is nearby. What about you girls? You're okay?"

"Yeah, we're fine," Samantha assured.

"Speak for your damn self, Samantha," Maggie said, chuckling.

"Don't pay any attention to Maggie. We're good. Besides, I'm driving."

"Okay, I'll see you gals at the diner," Jordan said. They got into their cars and drove two blocks to an all night diner. A waitress took their orders for coffee and returned quickly. "Shadow was lit back there tonight," Maggie said.

"Yes, it was a lot of fun," Jordan said.

"We even managed to get a nice invite to that upcoming party. I'll bet that is going to be the bomb," Samantha said.

"Damn," Maggie said, "I had such a nice little buzz going on leaving Shadow but it's nowhere to be found now."

They chatted and laughed while having their coffee.

After Jordan drank the last of her coffee she said, "Ladies, I'm going to head in. Got some things I want to do in the morning, so I'm going to say good night."

"Yeah, I need to be getting home also," Samantha said, finishing her coffee. They paid the bill and left, going off in different directions.

Jordan was enjoying the music on her radio when she turned onto her street and saw flashing lights on an ambulance across the street from her house. "Mrs. Irene," she said and pressed down on the accelerator. Jordan parked in her driveway. She turned off the engine, jumped out of her car and ran across the street where the ambulance was parked in Mrs. Irene's driveway. She rushed up the steps, the front door was open and she entered. "Mrs. Irene," she called out, rushing towards the bedroom. She was met at the bedroom door by one of the ambulance attendants. "What's going on?" She asked. "Is Mrs. Irene okay?"

"Who are you, ma'am?" The attendant asked, holding a pad and pen in his hand.

"I'm Jordan Banks. I live across the street." Her voice shook from the nervousness she was experiencing. "Mrs. Irene is a dear friend who's like family," she explained.

"We got a call. It appears this lady," he nodded in Mrs. Irene's direction, where she lay, with her eyes closed, on a gurney, "was experiencing some breathing issues and she called in." As he spoke, the other attendant checked Mrs. Irene's vitals and adjusted the fluid they'd hooked her up to.

"May I speak with her," Jordan asked.

"You can try but she's sort of out of it and she may not be very responsive."

Jordan rushed to the gurney. She'd never seen Mrs. Irene look so small and fragile before. "Mrs. Irene, how are you feeling?" She asked but Mrs. Irene didn't respond. She looked at the attendant and asked, "Is she going to be alright? When I checked on her earlier, she appeared to be fine."

"We're going to take her over to Doctor's Hospital on Wheeler. Does she live here alone?" the attendant inquired.

"Yes she does. Her only son lives in New York. I will call him."

"Did you want to follow us to the hospital?"

"Yes," Jordan said, not taking into consideration the way she was dressed, coming from an evening out with the girls.

When the attendants rolled Mrs. Irene out to the ambulance, Jordan walked beside her, holding her hand. She'd known Mrs. Irene a very long time but had never remember her being sick, and that frightened her.

"Mrs. Irene, they are going to take you to the hospital and will take good care of you."

"I'm alright," Mrs. Irene responded and that made Jordan feel better. "I just got this pain in my chest and I was having trouble breathing so I called 9-1-1."

"I'm glad you did. I'll follow you to the hospital and I'll call Brad on the way."

"Okay. Grab my medical information, please. You know where it is."

Mrs. Irene had always made sure Jordan knew where she kept her insurance and other important papers in the event such a situation occurred.

Obtaining the necessary records, Jordan locked the door , rushed back to her car and followed the ambulance to the hospital. She called Brad on the way.

"I'll be on the first flight out," he said.

Then Jordan called Steffie and Stevie.

When Jordan arrived at the hospital, she put on a sweater that she kept on the back seat in her car. She exited the car, rushed into the Emergency Room and provided the medical staff with Mrs. Irene's insurance information and answered their questions.

That completed, Jordan walked over to an available chair, she sat and waited for some word from the hospital staff.

Not more than fifteen minutes had passed when Steffie and Stevie enter the room, walked over to Jordan and took a seat on either side of her. Jordan informed them of what little she knew, and they waited for some information.

After a while, Steffie went to the restroom, leaving her phone on her chair next to Jordan. A few minutes later, her phone rang. Jordan looked towards the bathroom. She didn't see Steffie so she picked up the phone and answered it. "Hello."

Immediately, the call disconnected.

Jordan and Stevie talked among each other and after a while, he looked at Jordan and asked, "That dude ain't still harassing you, is he?"

"I'm so done with that!"

"I'm glad because he's not the man you thought he was. I don't know whether you know this but the word on the street about him ain't good."

"What are you talking about?" Jordan looked at Stevie with raised eyebrows.

"I hear that my man is dealing, heavily."

"Drugs?!"

"That's the word."

"Do you think it's true?"

"His name keeps popping up in that regard."

"You never said anything."

"There wasn't much to say besides since you were with the guy, I figured he couldn't be all bad."

"Well, think again. He's an asshole."

"I'm right there with you."

Jordan shook her head. "I just want him to keep his broke down ass away from me."

Steffie returned and Jordan handed her the phone. "You got a call but they hung up when I answered."

"Really?" She checked the number of the missed call. Then, asked, "Nothing yet?"

"No," Jordan answered.

"Y'all want something to drink?" Stevie asked, getting up to stretch his legs.

"I'm good," Jordan said.

Steffie shook her head.

Stevie was about to go to check out the snack machine when a medical professional came out, "The family of Irene Caughman."

Jordan, Steffie and Stevie rushed up to the doctor and Jordan said, "We're here for Mrs. Caughman. Her son will be coming in from New York soon."

"I'm Dr. Simpson," he said. "I'm sorry to say that Mrs. Caughman didn't make it."

"What?" Stevie asked, frowning.

"What are you saying, Doctor?" Jordan wasn't sure she initially understood what the doctor meant, but the telling look on his face told her everything. She knew then she had to exercise strength, not only for herself but her siblings. She couldn't let them see her fall apart. "You're not saying Mrs. Irene is dead?"

"Yes. I'm so sorry for your loss."

"What happened?" Jordan asked, unsteady on her feet and feeling as though she would faint. Tears quickly filled her eyes and she tried to brush them away but was unsuccessful before they began to flow down her cheeks.

Stevie placed his arms around her for support.

"Can we get you some water, Miss Banks?" The doctor offered.

"No, thanks," Jordan uttered, pulling tissues from her purse and wiped her cheeks. She looked from Stevie to Steffie, trying to make sure they were alright. "Can you tell us what happened, Dr. Simpson?" Stevie asked, devastated.

"Mrs. Caughman died a short while ago of a massive coronary. She suffered an attack prior to arriving at the hospital and another afterward. We worked on her but her heart gave out and there wasn't anything else we could do," he explained.

"I can't believe Mrs. Irene's gone," Steffie said, her voice tearful.

"Neither can I," Stevie said softly.

"Let us know if we can do anything for you and again, I'm very sorry for your loss." Dr. Simpson shook hands with Stevie, he excused himself and returned through the double doors that led to the emergency patients' section.

Steffie said, "I can't believe this. Mrs. Irene is gone. This can't be real." Then she looked at Jordan. "I hadn't seen her in a little while but when I last saw her, she seemed fine. What happened? Did she get sick?"

Jordan shook her head and said, "No. I saw her earlier today and she appeared to be fine." She closed her eyes and fought back tears that threatened to flow out of her eyes. "Are you two okay?" She asked Stevie and Steffie.

"I'm okay," Stevie said. "What about you girls?"

"I'm not okay at all," Steffie said.

"I don't know what I'm gonna do without her." Jordan choked back her tears. "How are we gonna tell Brad?"

"Have you heard anymore from him?" Stevie asked.

"He called once. I was surprised because he doesn't deal well with bad news. He goes into shut down mode, turns off his phone. I knew we wouldn't hear further from him until he was here. He's getting a flight out in the morning."

"We'll meet him at the airport," Steffie said, on the verge of tears.

"Yeah," Jordan said, trying to suppress her sobs, then she said, "This is gonna devastate him."

"I know," Stevie agreed as his voice cracked. He looked at Jordan. "You don't always have to be the strong one, Jordan. And, don't worry about Steffie and me. We'll be alright. We've got each other."

Jordan looked up into her brother's face and all she could think at that moment was how fortunate she was to have him and Steffie in her life. "I don't know how we're gonna tell Brad that his mom is dead? How are we gonna do that?" she said and could no longer hold back her tears, she began to cry.

Stevie wrapped his arms around his sisters and in the hospital Emergency Room, the three of them huddled together, and they wept.

CHAPTER 9

The following day, Jordan and the twins met Brad at the airport. When he saw them, without a word being spoken, they watched his smile fade. It was obvious Brad sensed the worst case scenario, and he was correct. After a long painful embrace, Stevie drove them to Mrs. Irene's house where, Jordan and Steffie made breakfast that they picked at, drank coffee, talked and cried. At the end of the day, Brad insisted that they all spend the night together.

Over the next few days, they assisted Brad in planning every aspect of Mrs. Irene's service, including the receiving of guests, and when Brad asked Jordan to speak on behalf of the family, she readily accepted. Jordan and Mrs. Irene had always been very close. She always said Jordan was like the daughter she never had, and though Jordan loved her equally and would do anything for Mrs. Irene, she knew that request would be a difficult one. And, as expected, the day of the services was one

of the worse days of Jordan's life. In church, the three sat next to Brad, Stevie, between his sisters, holding their hands. As various ones spoke very fine words about Mrs. Irene, nonstop tears crept from Jordan's lids and snaked down her cheeks. It took every ounce of strength for her to not leap from her seat and beg Mrs. Irene to not leave her. Steffie removed several tissues from her purse and handed them to Jordan.

When it was Jordan's turn to speak, Stevie walked with her up to the podium and she knew he wouldn't leave her side until she had done what was asked of her. She cleared her throat, her mouth quivered. She looked towards the ceiling, she cleared her throat again and silently asked God for strength. "I have always thought of Mrs. Irene as a second mother," she began, sharing the importance of Mrs. Irene in her and her siblings' lives, the impact she had on their decisions and the sacrifices she made on their behalf. Jordan felt as if she were floating on clouds as she talked about many things that endeared Mrs. Irene to her. At the end of her remarks, she said, "Mrs. Irene and I would have long talks; we talked about everything; poetry, art, music, sewing, life, even death. She always encouraged us to pursue our goals, go after what we want, and how tragic it would be to end an American dream without first pursuing it. Don't have regrets or live in the past, she often said, that the past only explains how we got here but the future is where we go from here. She would say, this is your life, wake up and pay attention. I don't know..." Jordan sniffed and brushed away tears as she looked over at the casket resting on a pedestal near where she stood. "I don't know what I'm going to do without you, Mrs. Irene. I miss you, I love you, and I will pay attention."

Before Stevie walked her back to her seat, they paused as she kissed her fingers and touched the casket. As Jordan and Stevie approached their seats, Brad and Steffie stood and the four of them embraced.

After the services concluded and they left the cemetery, family and friends gathered at Mrs. Irene's house. Samatha and Maggie assisted Jordan and Steffie, assuring that everyone was served refreshments. Later, the dispersed. Maggie and Samantha were the last to leave, and Brad, Jordan, Steffie and Steven were left alone. They laughed between tears as they recalled stories of growing up, the trouble Brad and Stevie got themselves into when they'd created some mischief and thought they'd gotten away with but realized later that they hadn't because Steffie had rat them out. She was a hot mess, they always said.

"Those were the days," Stevie laughed.

"Yeah," Brad agreed, laughing also.

"That was so much fun," Steffie said. We had a blast."

"Yeah right! Until you got involved," Stevie said to Steffie. "Then, the cat was out of the bag."

Jordan agreed. "Steffie would tell your business in a skinny minute. She definitely was that girl."

"She couldn't keep a doggone thing," Brad put in, "unless it was something she wanted to keep private. Everyone else's business was fair game.

"That was our Steffie alright," Jordan said, laughing.

"Was I really that bad?" Steffie asked, laughing.

"YES!" Jordan, Stevie and Brad said in unison.

They chuckled some more.

After a moment, Brad spoke. "Thank you, guys so much for all you did. I appreciate you all so much."

"No problem, Brad," Jordan assured him.

"Of course. Glad we could help," Steffie said, she got up and left the room.

"No problem, man," Stevie said. "Whatever you need."

After a few minutes, Steffie returned with a lit joint that she took a hit of before passing it on to Brad and taking her seat on the couch between Stevie and Jordan.

Sometime later, the Banks went home, leaving Brad to have some time to himself.

CHAPTER 10

The following day, Jordan and the twins drove Brad to the airport for his return to New York. On Friday night, Maggie and Samantha picked up Jordan and they went to Shadow. Jordan said, "I'd forgotten about the birthday party tonight."

"I don't doubt that. You've been through a lot this summer and summer ain't even over yet," Maggie commented, pulling away from a stop light. "But, how you went up there and spoke at Mrs. Irene's services, I'll never know. That couldn't have been easy."

"No, it wasn't easy but I would have done anything for Brad and Mrs. Irene."

"It may not seem like it right now but it'll get easier," Samantha assured her but it didn't feel that way for Jordan. "It was a beautiful service. I'm sure Mrs. Irene would've been very pleased." Then she said, "Girls, my laptop went out and it won't be repaired until Monday, but I need to do a little work over the weekend. Can either of you help a sista out? I refuse to buy another computer right now."

"Yeah. Stevie gave me one of his so you can borrow it," Jordan offered.

"Okay, I'll pick it up tomorrow afternoon."

They entered the semi-dark club. It was packed, the party in full swing, and the birthday boy was on the dance floor, locked in a kiss with a girl wearing a tight, red dress and matching stilettos. The club was alive, dancing, partygoers engaged in lively conversations while others were laughing, hanging out and getting their drink on.

Jordan, Samantha and Maggie greeted the birthday boy with birthday wishes and embraces and afterwards, they found available stools at the huge bar that took up one side of the club and they sat and ordered drinks that arrived shortly. After a short time, the three hit the dance floor and were soon joined by nicely dressed, handsome young men and they mixed it up vigorously on the dance floor.

Later, a birthday cake with lit candles was rolled out on a table draped in a white linen tablecloth. With a glass of champagne in each guest's hand, they toasted the lucky young man and sang happy birthday to him, he made a wish, the cake was cut and shortly afterwards, most of the guests returned to the dance floor.

At the end of the evening, they left the club with Jordan having had more to drink than she was accustomed. Maggie drove her home and she and Samantha insisted on walking Jordan to her door.

"This is not necessary," Jordan assured them, unhooking her seatbelt.

"You know you can't drink," Maggie grinned, getting out of her car. "Light weight."

The ladies saw Jordan safely inside before they waved goodbye and left. Jordan stood inside her front door and stared across the street at Mrs. Irene's house. A moment later, brushing tears from her face, she closed the door and staggered across the room, dropping her purse and keys on the coffee table before heading toward the bathroom, unzipping her dress and kicking off her shoes. As her dress fell to the floor, simultaneously the doorbell rang. She stepped out of the dress. "What did those two bird heads forget?" She staggered back towards the door. "What do you want? You've already gotten me drunk tonight."

She reached for the door knob. "Oh, you came back for the laptop?" She flung open the door and got the surprise of her life. Frank was standing there with flowers in his hands and a big silly grin on his face. "What are you doing here?!"

"I heard about Mrs. Irene," he said.

"Yeah, she's gone," she replied and overwhelmed again, she begun to cry.

Frank crossed over the threshold and quickly reached for Jordan. He was surprised at how easily and willingly she went into his arms. In her numb thought processes, she wasn't sure why she didn't slam the door in Frank's face. Was her reaction to his surprise visit the result of her pain at losing Mrs. Irene, was it the drinks she'd consumed earlier, or was she still in love with him. She was so overwhelmed and felt she needed someone, and Frank was there. Of all the possibilities, it could've been that she desperately missed Toby, knew she'd have to spend the rest of her life without him and that thought was too much to bear? It could have been any of the above or all of them. She wasn't sure and at that moment, damn it, she didn't care. Frank didn't care either. Jordan was exactly where he wanted her to be. She was in his arms and that was the only thing he cared about.

In one swift moment, Frank kicked the door shut, dropped the bouquet of flowers on the floor and wrapped his arms tightly around Jordan, and they began kissing, passionately, clawing at each other. He lifted her from the floor and with her arms wrapped around his neck, he carried her to her bedroom, and locked in a heated embrace with the thought of satisfying their needs, they fell on her bed together.

When he was able to tear his mouth from hers, he said hoarsely, "Baby, I'm so sorry for what I did. Please forgive…," he begun but Jordan's hand went up to his mouth to interrupt whatever he was trying to say.

"I don't want to talk. Please let's not talk," she said, then she covered his mouth with hers, stabbing her tongue deep inside his mouth. Their mouths devoured each other's. Their kisses grew deeper, filled with passion, so much passion.

When they pulled apart, he said, "I missed the hell outta you, baby. I missed you so damn much."

"Please," she whispered into his mouth." "Please."

Jordan was suffering from overwhelming pain, so much loss so quickly. Mrs. Irene was lost to her, gone forever. And Toby, he was lost to her also. She knew she had lingering feelings in her head and her heart for Toby. She would never forget that one special day that they spent together, it was paradise, but it was obvious he didn't feel the same. Then, there was Frank who she'd loved a long time, but he'd betrayed her in the worse way. Jordan knew it would take a lot for her to trust Frank again, if she ever would. But right now, she just wanted what he could give to pull her from that dark, lonely pit she found herself in and make her feel better. That was as far as she could see right now and that was all she wanted to see.

Frank kneeled on the floor beside the bed. He caught Jordan's legs, dragged her body until her legs dangled over the side of the bed, and he nestled between them. In lightning quickness, he removed her bra and panties, cast them to the floor and he feasted on her breasts, pleasuring them equally before a trail of wet kisses moved quickly to her navel, then beyond. When his opened mouth connected with the juncture between her thighs, her hands grasp the back of his head and held him there. He lifted her hips from the bed so that his mouth could move deeper into her hollow vessel, her most intimate spot. Once there, he shoved his tongue in and out of her. He kissed her, licked her, sucked her, and he drank from her, all of her sweetness.

After a while, Frank moved from the floor, yanked his short sleeve sweater over his head and kicked out of his shoes and slacks. In the next second, he moved on top of her and when their bodies were perfectly aligned, he shoved his long, thick member into her with such force that she screamed. Jordan was tipsy but she was certain the name she screamed out wasn't Frank's. Had Frank been too high to notice or was he unwilling to acknowledge what he knew he heard because he wanted her so badly? With her legs wrapped tightly around his waist and him grinding fiercely into her, she responded recklessly.

Sometime later, they fell apart, drenched in perspiration.

"With all that's happened around us, there's still that pull between us," Frank said. "It's like a raging fire burning out of control and neither one of us can stop it—or even want to stop it. You know that, don't you?" He asked, confidently with Jordan neatly tucked in his arms again.

"I'm tired and I just want to sleep," she said, moving out of his embrace, she turned her back to him and fell into a deep sleep.

Jordan felt she'd just closed her eyes when she was awakened by Frank mounting her again. Not so tipsy now, she questioned whether she was making a mistake being with him again and that question persisted all during the night as Frank pounded away at her, draining her of her bodily fluids.

CHAPTER 11

That Saturday morning, the impatient ringing of the front doorbell jarred Jordan out of a deep sleep. It took a moment for her head to clear, and she remembered that Samantha was coming to pick up the laptop.

Frank's face was cradled in the curve of Jordan's neck, his alcoholic breath, warm on her shoulder. She checked the time on the clock on the night table. Seven thirty. She wiggled out of Frank's arms and climbed out of bed, slipping on her robe. She was happy during the night that she'd asked Frank to park his motorcycle in the garage. She wouldn't have to explain his presence to her friends.

When the doorbell rang again, heading barefooted towards her office, Jordan called out, "Just a minute, Sam."

Jordan hurriedly grabbed the old laptop from the desk, raced to the front door and flung it open. She froze in her track, the laptop fell from her hands to the floor with a crash as she stared into dark simmering eyes surrounded by thick lush lashes. She felt her entire body tremble, her heart missed a beat and the deep heavy thud in her chest took her breath away, making her weak and dizzy. Tobin Douglas!

"Yes, it's me," he said, smiling as he bent down to retrieve the laptop.

Jordan stared at him, unable to believe her eyes. Toby was standing there. As she stared into the eyes of the man whom she thought was lost to her forever, everything else around her cease to exist. She wanted to go to him willingly, happily, but as her mind began to catch up with reality, her happiness seeing him was quickly replaced with anger. Why hadn't he contacted her as he said he would?! Why had he waited so long to come to her?!

"Good morning." His eyes sparkled at seeing her, his mouth widened into that devastatingly handsome smile that she remembered so well and loved so much.

At first, Jordan couldn't speak, couldn't tear her gaze away from his as electricity passed between them and raced non-stop through her body. "Toby," she was finally able to whisper. Her voice trembled and she felt weak in her knees. "What are you doing here? I didn't think I'd ever see you again."

He threw his head back and laughed as he entered the room and closed the door behind him, placing the laptop on the coffee table. His gaze sweep over Jordan, keenly observing how her robe clung to her shapely body and fell open at her throat, exposing creamy flesh between her breasts. Toby felt happiness exploding inside him, more happiness than he felt since they first met. He wanted to gather her in his arms, hold her tight and never let her out of his sight again. Ever!

"Never see me again?" He tilted his head to one side and gave her a smile that sent shock waves through her body. "Are you serious?" He moved closer to her, but she raised one hand up against his chest to stop him. He obeyed, but asked, "Do you remember what we talked about before we parted?" He didn't wait for her to answer, he continued, "I told you then that I was in love with you. I was in love with you then. I'm in love with you right now. That hasn't changed.   If anything, my love for you has grown since I saw you last. I can't get you out of my mind, baby. You're there." He tapped the side of his head with his fingers. "Day and night." Jordan looked at him. He couldn't tell whether that look was still the shock at seeing him again or disbelief in what he was saying. "I love you, baby."

"You say you love me, but I haven't heard from you since I left the island. I thought you forgot about me or that you decided we'd just be friends and leave it at that," she said in hushed tones, his nearness making swallowing difficult. "And when I didn't hear…" She paused as her voice shook. Here Toby was, standing in her living room, looking good wearing the hell out of an expensive gray lightweight suit and white shirt, right down to his black Tanino Crisci shoes. "When I didn't hear from you, I didn't know what to think."

"Why are we whispering?" he said with laughter in his voice. "Darling, I always knew I wasn't gonna let you go. I've just been so busy."

Jordan couldn't believe he had the nerve to laugh about being too busy to contact her when all she thought about was him. She took a deep breath and in a calm voice, she began, "So let me get this right. You were too busy to call, text or send me an email?" she spat out, her lips quivering. "You chose to do nothing."

Jordan was furious now. If Toby had reached out to her, she wouldn't have been so vulnerable and allowed Frank back into her life, not even for one night.

Toby ran his fingers through her long lustrous locks. "I was doing things that I wanted to share with you," he said, excitedly looking at the woman who'd managed to capture his heart in a single day. His eyes danced like those of a mischievous young boy who pulled off a devious stunt without getting caught. "You have no idea how long I've waited for this moment, to look into your beautiful eyes, hold you in my arms, say all the things that I want to say to you. Make love to you." As he spoke, his mouth descended closer to hers. "I came for you, Jordan. I came for you. I want you."

"You think you can come here now and…," Jordan began, angrily before Toby pulled her roughly into his arms and silenced her with a kiss that was passionate, full of fire. He stabbed his tongue into her mouth and began probing, searching, commanding, demanding. At first, she struggled to free herself but the intensity of his kiss increased with a raw hunger, a hunger that caused her knees to buckle and her senses to reel.

Jordan realized Toby held the kind of power that clouded her thoughts, set her body ablaze and stir rampant emotions in her that were far from friendly. He kissed her, not holding anything back. Her body sagged against his. All the fight she'd held on to for weeks was now gone, she began kissing him back with passion, responding to pure human desire, sheer unbridled need, her own animalistic want. Jordan became lost in the kiss; the intensity, the pleasure.

She was with Toby! This was no dream. He was actually there with her. It was real! They were holding each other, kissing each other and that meant everything!

She kissed him with a thorough passion that even she didn't know she possessed; she sucked on his lips, jabbed her tongue further into his mouth, then easing his mouth further into hers, while all sense of reasoning escaped her. Through her robe, Toby cupped her breasts, his finger gently teasing them. He broke the kiss to gaze into her beautiful, lust-filled eyes. He rubbed his thumb over her kissed swollen lips. Slowly his gaze moved to her beautiful cleavage. His eyes lingered on the hardened nipples pressing tightly against her robe, and his mind could only think of what lay under the thin fabric. He wanted her so badly! Was her body waiting for him to claim? Could he claim her as his own? Toby could never remember wanting anyone or anything as much as he wanted Jordan.

"I've waited so long for this," he said.

Toby was desperate to tear off Jordan's robe with his teeth, wrap his mouth around her ripened, inviting nipples and torture them with his tongue, his mouth until she begged him to never stop! She was poised, eager as he bent his head to kiss her again.

"Jordan!" A male voice suddenly erupted, pulling them from the passionate state they were locked in before Toby could make his desires for her become a sweet reality.

A frown creased Toby's forehead as he and Jordan simultaneously turned in the direction from where the voice had come. Frank! Jordan stiffened as reality slowly seeped into the deep recesses of her mind. Jordan had completely forgotten there was a naked man in her bed. An agonizing wave of dread washed over her, followed by a cold chill that made her shiver.

"Baby, where are you?" Frank called out again. "Bring that fine ass back to bed."

Jordan gulped in a deep breath of air when Frank appeared in the living room with a sheet covering his body from the waist down.

"I need more of your good lov...." Frank began but the rest of his words froze inside his mouth as he caught sight of Jordan wrapped in the arms of another man. "What the hell is going on here?" It didn't take a rocket scientist to figure out what was going on between Jordan and Toby, but Frank demanded to know anyway, approaching them aggressively. His eyes darted from one to the other before he exploded. "Who the fuck are you?"

Jordan swallowed hard and moved out of Toby's embrace. Frank, extremely jealous, was unpredictable. She never knew what he might do in a situation such as that, since she knew he often reacted to situations without thinking.

Recognizing the look in Frank's eyes and knowing it wasn't good, Jordan avoided eye contact with either man and casted her eyes away, making the introductions. "Frank, this is Tobin Douglas. Toby, Frank Benjamin."

"Who are you, dude?" Frank demanded.

Jordan responded. "Toby and I met when I was in Jamaica."

A cold, hard knot formed in Toby's chest. So this is Frank, he thought as his gaze shifted from Frank back to Jordan. The picture of her standing there in a sheer robe that clung to a body underneath that was so curvy to be sinful and Frank coming out of her bedroom wrapped only in a sheet, painted a picture for Toby, a painfully clear picture. He knew only too well what'd been going on between Jordan and Frank before his arrival and his heart felt sick with that knowledge.

Frank folded his arms across his chest and glared at Toby, but he directed his question at Jordan. "Okay, if you met this dude in Jamaica, why the hell is he here?"

Toby stepped around Jordan. The warm eyes that greeted her earlier were no longer present. They'd clouded over and turned cold, as they glared back at Frank. "Not that it's any of your business," Toby said, "but I came here for Jordan."

"If it's about Jordan, it damn sure is my business, bro," Frank said, uncrossing his arms, his hands forming huge fists at his side.

The air was electric with tension. It was clear that neither man was intimidated by the other and at any second, a serious fight could erupt, and that was the last thing Jordan wanted.

Frank was a man from the streets, had a military background and always acted tough, but she also knew that Toby had earned a number of awards in Kung Fu. As the two men advanced towards each other, Jordan quickly moved in between them. "Stop it, you two. You're behaving like teenagers," she said, glancing from one man to the other, still trembling from the after affects of Toby's kisses.

"I should throw his ass out of here," Frank sneered.

Toby raised his brow at that. "You could always try," he challenged.

"I don't know who you think you are coming up in here like you own something. Jordan belongs to me. So don't get it twisted, my friend. She is mine! All mine!" Frank hurled at Toby, jerking his thumb towards his chest.

"Keep telling yourself that," Toby countered, as maddeningly confident as he was feeling.

"What you don't seem to understand is that Jordan and I have history. Three years." Frank raised three fingers to emphasize his point. "What about you? One week?" He raised one finger. "Now, you really can't compare the two, can you?"

"Actually, it was more like one day." Toby raised one finger to mimic Frank and tilted his head to one side with a hint of a smile on his face.

Jordan interceded. "I'm no one's property," she made clear to both men. "I don't belong to anyone!"

Ignoring Jordan's comment, Frank gave Toby a threateningly stare. "Look bro, I think you've said about enough."

"Really?" Toby was sarcastic, folding his arms across his chest and scowling at Frank.

"What are you gonna do now—fight?!" Again Jordan looked from one man to the other. "Are you two insane?"

"Don't worry, sweetheart. That cat is definitely not ready for this jungle," Toby said to Jordan, while looking directly into Frank's eyes with confidence and a smile on his handsome, calm face.

"Sweetheart?!" Frank objected and made a move toward Toby.

"Frank!" Jordan pushed against his chest and pointing toward the bedroom door, said, "You get dressed. I need to speak to Toby. Alone!" When Frank made no attempt to leave, she hissed, "Go get dressed! Now!"

Frank hesitated. Then, said, unhappily, "Yeah," pointing a finger towards Toby's face sneering, "but I ain't going nowhere, buddy! Believe that!" He stomped off towards the bedroom.

When Jordan and Toby were alone, she looked at everything in the room continuing to avoid his eyes. He placed his hands on her shoulders and turned her to face him. He asked, "Are you all right?"

Jordan was amazed that with all Toby had witnessed at her home that morning that he'd be concerned about her. "I don't know whether I'll ever be all right again."

"You had a life before we met. We've talked about that, but you've got to decide what you want. I know this is upsetting to you. Hell, it's upsetting to me as well, and I have to ask you, why are you back with that jerk?!"

Jordan was silent as she looked at Toby.

"He doesn't deserve you."

"It's complicated, Toby."

"Jordan, I came here because you and I found something in Jamaica, something special. I felt it then, I feel it now and I know you felt it too. So I'm here to see what we're gonna do about it."

"As I said, it's complicated."

"Not if you know what you want. I care about you. All I want to do is love you, take care of you, and if you want that too, I'll handle it from there." Toby gave Jordan a polite smile, but she knew that whatever 'handle it' meant, she was certain he meant just that. "I know you care about me. You couldn't have kissed me the way you did if you didn't. Tell me there's something between us." His eyes pleading as he stood and waited for an answer.

"When we were in Jamaica, you told me you loved me yet you returned to America and it appeared you forget about me. How do you expect me to feel or trust you?! I was going through hell. You knew that. I don't know what you expect from me now."

Jordan was overwhelmed with emotions. She was angry that Toby appeared to have abandoned her. And, after not giving into Frank's advances for weeks then suddenly fall into this situation just as Toby came and made his true feelings known, caused her blood to boil. She was tired of men making assumptions about her. This time, even if it meant her being hurt more, she intended to turn the tale around this time.

She couldn't help wondering why in the hell did Frank picked last night to bring his ass to her home? Why had she been so vulnerable and gave in to him? Why?! Why?! Why?! She wanted to scream.

"There's no excuse for the way I handled our situation," Toby began, "And, I'm not gonna make excuses for my behavior, but if you'll allow me to explain, I believe you will understand."

"Would you let me finish?! Please!" Jordan nearly screamed at Toby. Then, she said, "I was going through hell. My whole world had come crashing down around me and I felt lost. I can't even describe how much pain I was in. I had no idea how I was going to get through it all, and last night— well last night I needed someone and," she paused again, "well, Frank was there."

Toby grimaced. What a complete ass he'd been to not contact Jordan sooner.

"Frank made a mistake, he's ending his marriage and though there's a lot we have to discuss, we're going to see where it goes. He said he loves me and he wants me back."

Jordan felt she was in a whirlwind and didn't know which way to turn so she blurted out what was in her mind. Whether she wanted to hurt Toby as he had her, she'd never be sure. All she knew was that she'd never been in such a deep, dark place.

"Of course he wants you back. Why wouldn't he? He was a damn fool for leaving in the first place, but he did and I couldn't be happierd. Had he not done so, I probably would have never met you. But, the important thing right now is what do you want? He doesn't look like the kind of tiger that would change his stripes."

"Toby," Jordan said as her voice cracked, "Frank and I are going to give it another try. He made a mistake. He says he loves me and I believe him. You understand, don't you?" She looked pleadingly at him but the look on his face, the hurt in his eyes broke Jordan's heart. She closed her eyes and shook her head. When she opened her eyes again, she said, "It's difficult to just throw away three years."

Toby lifted Jordan's chin so he could look into her eyes. "Don't settle for less when you can have it all, Jordan. You deserve it all. That is a fool in there," Toby pointed toward Jordan's bedroom. "You don't need that in your life. You are better than that."

She wasn't sure about her own feelings anymore. She was confused. Was she still in love with Frank? Had she fallen in love with Toby? Disturbed by the ambivalence of her feelings, she turned away as tears formed in her eyes.

Jordan heard the front door open. When she turned back, she noticed Toby was gone. She walked over to the door, closed it and with her back against the door, she wondered why her life was so screwed up. Why couldn't she have a normal, happy life? She slid to the floor. "Why?" She screamed, slapping her hand against her forehead. Why had she allowed Frank back into her home and her life last night? Why?! She was smarter than that. Too smart to involve herself in a situation that she knew she no longer wanted or would ever repeat.

Frank came out of the bedroom fully dressed with a scowl on his face. "So that dude left huh? He shoulda never come here. Punk ass moth….." Seeing Jordan weeping, he stopped, rushed over to her and lifted her from the floor. She pushed his hands away. "Come here," he said, standing close to her. "What's wrong?"

"Just go, Frank. I need you to leave."

Frank stepped back and stared at her, a puzzled expression on his face. "Why? I thought you and I were getting back on track. Why would you want me to leave now? Does this have anything to do with that joker you sent packing." When Jordan didn't answer, he asked, "Is he boning you?"

"That's none of your business so stay in your fucking lane," Jordan hissed, furiously.

"I don't know why you're acting like this. Come on. Let's go back to bed."

"No!" She yelled. Then, she pulled together all the strength she always knew she had. "Don't you touch me! Don't ever touch me again. It is over, Frank! Over!"

"You said that before, remember?"

Jordan ignored that comment. "Don't call me and don't come here again." Her voice was crisp and decisive. She knew what Toby said was true. She did deserve better, so much better than Frank. She also knew she'd rather be alone and miserable the rest of her life than to live her life with the likes of Frank Benjamin. It wasn't worth it—Frank wasn't worth it.

"You don't mean that." He had the nerve to have a look of confidence on his face.

"Really?"

He took a step towards her.

"Get out, Frank."

Frank saw something in Jordan's face, telling him he shouldn't push his luck. He bit his inner cheek and stared at her a long moment before he turned, walked out and slammed the door shut behind him.

Alone now, she walked into her bedroom with a million and one thoughts rushing around inside her head. She began pacing around the room like a caged animal. Suddenly, she looked at her bed, the crumpled sheets and remembered what had happened there between her and Frank. She rushed to the bed, ripped of the sheets and took them to the washing machine.

She was having a cup of coffee when her doorbell rang. She went to the door and opened it. "Hey girl." Jordan stepped aside for Samantha to enter.

"I was hoping you weren't still in bed," Samantha said as she entered the house.

"You want some coffee or something?"

"No thanks. I just need to grab the laptop. Get home and get started on this report. I don't want to be slaving over the computer all day."

That was Jordan's cue to give Samantha the laptop and let her go since she had no intention of sharing the events of last night just yet. "I dropped it last night but I checked it out this morning and it's working fine."

She took the laptop from Jordan's hands. Then looking at her, she asked, "Are you okay, Jordan? You look like you've been crying."

"I just have a little headache. Too much to drink last night, I'm sure."

"Do you need anything?"

"No, I'm fine. Thanks!"

"Well, take a couple of aspirin and lie down a while."

"I think I'll do just that."

"Okay. Thanks for the use of the computer, and I'll see you at church tomorrow."

Jordan closed the door behind Samantha. She walked over to the couch, set her coffee cup on the table and sat where she had full view through the window of Mrs. Irene's house. She drew her feet up onto the couch, and with her knees up against her chest, she wrapped her arms around her legs and began to question her most recent behavior. What had gotten into her? She'd been behaving badly; spending the night in Jamaica with a stranger she'd just met on the beach, then last night, drinking more than usual, kissing one man while her bed was still warm from having had sex with another who was still sleeping in that warm space. She was behaving like a naive teenager. Even though her friends were experiencing sexual activities, some of whom had multiple partners, Jordan only had thoughts about those activities. Some of her friends who lost their virginity during their junior or senior year in high school, Jordan lost her virginity during her sophomore year in college and Frank had been the man she'd lost it too.

After high school, Frank had enlisted into the Army, had planned to make a career of it until he was injured in Flight School when he took his second jump.

Throughout the years, Jordan and Frank kept in touch. When on leave, he'd return home. Jordan had remained faithful to him, even though there were rumors that while on leave, Frank would come into town, sow his wild oats and return to his post without seeing her. She'd been so in love with him that she excused many things that he did.

"Why have I been so stupid all of my life?" She whispered. "Am I ever gonna get it right?" She wiped away tears that had started to flow down her face. "I miss you, Mrs. Irene. I don't know what I'm gonna do without you." Then, she settled back in the cushions on the couch and she wept.

CHAPTER 12

Jordan pulled from her bedroom closet bags of fabric, buttons, hooks, pins and piping that she took to the sewing room and placed on the sewing table. Within an hour, she'd cut out a number of items and before long, she was seated at her machine, sewing. It was much later when she finally pushed back from the sewing machine, exhausted and hungry. She rubbed her eyes, then she stretched, yawned and glanced at her watch. "Almost midnight," Jordan said, musing what she'd have for dinner.

Within minutes, she sat and had a bowl of Frosted Flakes. She poured a glass of wine that she took to her bedroom. After taking a shower and putting on her pajamas, she had her wine and she went to bed.

Unable to sleep, Jordan tossed and turned most of the night. Her mind was in a blaze about Toby. At the dawn of a brand new day, she got out of bed, pulled from her dresser drawer a pair of shorts and a top that she put on. After she laced up her running shoes, she left her house.

Why had she sent Toby away? He came for her, assuring her that he was in love with her and he wanted to be with her. This is what she'd waited for months for. Why didn't she allow him to stay? She thought they met, enjoyed each other's company and when she left the island, it was over and Toby would move on. She thought he'd forgotten about her. And, after not giving into Frank's advances for weeks, he suddenly comes over and she falls into his arms and it happens just as Toby comes to her and makes his feelings known.

Why had Frank picked that particular night to show up at her house, especially when she was most venerable? Why?!   She was angry at Toby, angrier at Frank but she was angriest at herself.

After Jordan's run and she arrived back home, she still felt stressed. She went into the kitchen, pulled a bottle of water from the refrigerator and took several sips from it. She later took a shower, she went into the living room and picked up a magazine that she leafed through. Before long, she yawned, placed the magazine back on the table, and she climbed back into bed. She stared up at the ceiling and thought about how her life had torpedoed so far out of control. At that point, there wasn't anything about her life that was happy. She was miserable, and she was alone.

After a while and still unable to sleep, Jordan got out of bed and went into the kitchen. She removed a quart of chocolate ice cream from the freezer, she fished a tablespoon from the drawer and after removing the lid from the container, she began shoving spoonfuls of the delicious frozen chocolate into her mouth. She spooned more ice cream into her mouth as she returned to her bed. She picked up the TV remote from the night stand and turned on the TV. She saw nothing of interest and turned the TV off and put the radio on. She then settled back against the pillows with her legs tucked underneath her and enjoyed listening to music and eating ice cream.

Sometime later, she fell asleep, but it was frothed with nightmares about Toby and Frank. Hours later, she woke and was annoyed, seeing that she'd not returned the uneaten portion of the ice cream to the freezer. "Damn," Jordan said. The ice cream had melted into a chocolate mess, ran down the side of the night table and had settled into a puddle on the floor. She got out of bed, went to the bathroom and returned with some wet hand towels and a trash can to clean up the mess.

After dumping everything into the outside garbage, Jordan returned to the kitchen with the newspaper that she spread out on the kitchen table and read while having cereal and milk and juice for breakfast before she got dressed and drove to church.

The minister delivered his message. It was about *loss*. He talked about everyone experiencing loss in their lives but it was vital that we not allow loss to define us, and that through the will of God, we should force ourselves to recover from that loss, move forward and prosper with our lives.

"We're aware that the choir's anniversary is coming up in August and we were thinking about getting new robes," the minister said. "We no longer have a designated person to drive our fund raising efforts for that project since we lost Mrs. Irene. We will continue to pray, trust, and work hard towards our goal."

"Amen," the parishioners said in unison.

After church, Jordan spoke with some of the members and as the minister and First Lady exited the church, she approached them and they spoke a few minutes before she drove home.

In her bedroom, Jordan removed the pink suit and black leather high heels, replacing them with a short sleeve blouse and shorts. She took a bottle of water from the fridge, went into the sewing room and emptied a large basket of fabrics, threads, basting materials, measuring tapes, and she spent most of the afternoon sewing.

Sometime later, she ate chicken salad on a bed of lettuce, sliced tomatoes, cucumbers and she had a glass of lemonade. After a while, she went into the living room and just as she sat on the couch, her phone vibrated. Thinking it was Frank calling again, as he'd done numerous times since that horrible night that went unanswered by her. She even hoped it was Toby. It was neither. She snatched up the phone. "Hello, Mrs. Benjamin," she said, not blaming her for mistakes her son made.

"Jordan, how have you been, dear?" Sarah Benjamin asked with genuine interest.

"I'm okay."

"I'm surprised I haven't heard from you. Frank told me he's getting his marriage annulled and that he wants you back. What do you think about that?"

"Mrs. Benjamin, what Frank does now is of no interest to me. I suggest he try to make his marriage work."

"He said the two of you spent a night together recently. Is that true?" She asked and Jordan could sense glee in her voice.

"I'm sorry but I'm not going to discuss anything about your son except to say that he and I are done."

"Jordan, my son loves you. Why would you want to break his heart?"

Had Sarah Benjamin forgotten how Frank ripped her heart to shreds? "Frank and I aren't good for each other."

"But you've always loved Frank. And, I know he loves you. The way Frank went about things was wrong and I know he has regrets, but I think you two oughta give it another try. I don't think you'd be sorry."

Jordan shook her head. "Nice talking with you, Mrs. Benjamin. Take care of yourself." Jordan hung up.

She wasn't sure why she'd allowed Frank into her home again after the way he treated her. Perhaps, it was because her mother behaved that way. Growing up, she watched men abuse her mother and she allowed them to come back. Was this part of a family cycle? Was she destined to follow in her mother's footsteps? Her mother would dress in her finest clothes, go out and in the early morning hour, would return with some man. Jordan would hear the man beat the crap out of her, hear her screams and in the next minute, she'd hear them having wild, raw sex, talking dirty to each other and howling in drunken laughter. After a while, she'd hear her mother being hit again, followed by her violent screams. Later, Jordan would hear the door slammed, her mother crying again and left to deal with her emotional and physical pain, alone. It always disappointed Jordan that her mother would allow those same abusers to return for a second or third round of abuse. Perhaps her mother allowed the mistreatment, the abuse because she didn't believe she deserved better.

Jordan bolted upright in her seat, startled by the realization. Toby was absolutely right, she thought. She certainly did deserve better than what she'd gotten from Frank. From this moment forward, she decided with renewed determination that she'd demand better and she'd have better. Since last seeing Toby, she couldn't stop thinking what he was doing. Was he seeing anyone? Was he hurt by what he found going on between her with Frank? Did he file that situation away as an 'oh well' moment and moved on? There were questions that kept rolling around inside her head. Did Toby ever love her? Did he still love her? Jordan had felt safe with Toby, had never felt more secure with anyone as she did with him. Her anger returned and she called Frank.

"Hello, baby," he answered, happy that she finally returned his call. Jordan could hear music in the background and knew he was at some bar, drinking and living it up. That was what he did. "I wasn't sure I'd hear from you again."

As she listened, she thought she heard a familiar voice mingled amongst the noises in the background. "Is that Steffie I hear?" She asked.

"Steffie? Why would you think Steffie is here?"

"Because I thought I heard her voice."

"Well, Steffie isn't here, but I'm glad that you finally returned my call."

Ignoring his comment, she said, "Look, I'm gonna make this simple and quick and it's not open for discussion. I just want you to hear me out."

"Okaaay," he dragged out the word.

"What happened the last time we were together was a mistake."

"But Jorda…" Frank tried to protest.

She cut him off. "Would you please just shut the fuck up and listen," she raised her voice. "It was a mistake, but I don't blame you completely. I was equally at fault, and I accept my responsibility in that bullshit, but you can be sure that under no circumstances will something like that ever happen again. I thought I needed something that I know with absolute certainty that I would be far better off without. I never should've allowed you back into my life after you treated me like shit, but that's water under the bridge. I don't need you in my life nor do I want you in my life and if you ever come near me again or call me, I will file a Restraining Order against your ass so damn fast it will make your head spin. And, stop filling your momma's head with a bunch of bullshit. It is over. Goodbye, Frank."

"You might be sorry for that decision," he said.

Jordan hung up. A short while ago, she was miserable thinking she'd spend the rest of her life without Frank, now, she felt a huge burden was lifted off her shoulders at the thought of never seeing his ass again. It was odd how things changed.

CHAPTER 13

Early that Tuesday afternoon, Jordan drove North on Hollandale Road to Oceana Park. She would go there often and sketch when the weather was nice. She parked her car, got out and entering the park, she came upon what appeared to be a perfect family of four; husband, wife, a little girl and boy. The children were running ahead of the adults; running, playing, having fun. How happy they looked. Jordan hadn't thought much about having children since she practically raised her sister and brother, but recently, she'd been giving more thought to getting married and having her own family.

Jordan came across a vacant bench. She sat, enjoying the fragrance of magnolia and jasmine mingling in the air. After a while, she pulled from her handbag, a sketch pad and pencils when a little boy riding a skateboard zoomed by. Suddenly, he fell and began to cry. Jordan quickly put her pad and pencils on the bench, jumped up and rushed to help the boy. A woman reached the young boy at the same time.

"Sweetheart, are you alright?" The woman asked, reaching for the boy.

"Is he okay?" Jordan inquired, looking from the boy to the woman.

"Mommy, I hurt myself," the boy cried.

The woman examined the small bruise on his leg. "It's just a little scrape," she said, soothingly to the boy. Then to Jordan, she added, "His little ego is probably more bruised than anything, but thank you."

"Sure," Jordan replied and waved to them as she walked away, returning to the bench to resume her sketching. Later, she gathered her things, got into her car and on the way home, she stopped off at Yolanda's Yogurt Shop to purchase a large cone of strawberry yogurt.

On Saturday morning, she awoke and lying in bed, she began to fantasizing about Toby. No matter how busy she was, she couldn't get him out of her mind. Her face broke out in a grin and she chuckled at the thought about Maggie's comment about bondage. The alarm buzzing on her phone jarred her back to reality. She went on an early run and returned later, dripping with perspiration. She waved to a neighbor as she picked up the newspaper from her lawn. She entered her house, got a bottle of water and as she drank, she looked out the kitchen window to observe two squirrels frolicking around the yard, then racing up a tree, one chasing after the other. Later, she changed into jeans and a blouse, went out back to get her gardening tools and she cleared flower beds, she did some weeding, adjusted pine needles around azaleas that were already in full bloom and turning on the sprinkler, her phone vibrated in her jean pocket. "What's up, "Stevie?" She answered, checking out the yard as she talked with her brother.

"I've got a little info for you. Seems your boy is running some major stuff through his welding business and he has a number of people on his payroll. There are other things I'm hearing, but I won't say anymore until I can check it out further."

"Wow. You never know what some people will do." Jordan said, slowly. "I just want him to leave me alone."

"He doesn't want me to bust him up."

"No, we're not doing anything like that," Jordan calmly said, not wanting to spike any further anger in her brother. "Be careful and stay as far away from him as you can."

The call ended and Jordan turned off the sprinkler. The sun was heading toward the center of the sky, the temperatures were rising, and the previous early morning breezes ceased to exist.

That afternoon, she picked up clothes from the cleaners, bought wine and went to the fabric shop and charged yards of fabric to her credit card, thankful that fabric was on sale. After a quick visit to her favorite book store and picking up a new bestseller, she returned home. Just before seven that evening, Samantha called. Something had come up and she wouldn't be able to attend a friend's pre-Fourth of July barbecue.

"Damn. I gotta go to Jackie's barbecue alone?" Jordan said.

"No big deal. You know practically everyone who'll be there," Samantha said.

"It won't be the same. First Maggie can't go and now you. It'll look odd if I don't show up."

"Just go, hang out, have a few drinks, then leave.

"I'll go but I won't enjoy it." They giggled.

Jordan arrived at Jackie's barbecue alone. She mingled, some of the kids talked her into playing some games with them, and she was later paired off with a man she had nothing with but she even laughed at his unfunny jokes. At about nine that night, Jordan thanked her hostess for the invite, she said goodbye to her and several others on her way out, and she drove home.

The next week, Jordan had completed the last of the bright red robes with a white collar and yellow trim. She laid the robes on the couch, stood back with her arms folded across her chest and admired her handiwork. Sunday morning, she arrived at church early and entered, carrying two bags that she set on a table in the Pastor's Study where she met with Rev. and First Lady Zeigler. "Good morning," she greeted them.

"Good morning, Jordan. It's always nice to see you," Mrs. Zeigler said and she and Rev. Zeigler embraced Jordan.

"It was so good of you to treat the choir with such an amazing gift, Sister Jordan. A wonderful blessing," Rev. Zeigler said. "I've asked them to assemble in the Fellowship Hall. They're going to be thrilled."

"Yes they will be," Mrs. Zeigler agreed.

Jordan pulled a robe from a bag and held it up so it could be viewed. That robe was greeted with lots of oooohs and ahhhhs as well as lots of gratitude from Rev and First Lady Zeigler. Jordan insisted that the minister and his wife present the choir with the robes, then they went into the Hall where the choir was waiting.

"This is fabulous, Jordan," one choir member complimented as she slipped into the new robe.

"I love it," another member said.

"You did an amazing job, Jordan. I can't believe how quickly you were able to make them," First Lady Zeigler said.

"Yes, an amazing job, Sister Jordan and we thank you very much," Rev. Zeigler said. Later, after the robes were viewed and put away, they all went into the sanctuary to begin Sunday morning services, Jordan took her seat, happy that the choir members would have new robes for their anniversary program in August, less than a month away. Before going to bed, she was surprised and delighted to see she'd received emails from both, Gina and Trish, they messaged a while, and she went to bed.

Jordan's mind was ablaze with thoughts; the changes in her life; the changes in the twins' lives, their recent independence. She felt they were probably in over their heads, buying such a costly home but they were living their lives as they choose, and they appeared to be happy.

It was then that Jordan decided she would stop procrastinating and pursue her own dream and she would begin that journey soon, very soon. She was grateful she was not moving closer to her goal, and she was happy with that thought.

It was daylight before Jordan fell into a deep sleep, but the last thought that floated inside her head were thoughts of Toby. "I love you, Toby. I love you so much. Please don't give up on me. Don't give up on us."

CHAPTER 14

Summer dragged on intermittently. Jordan did everything she could to keep busy and keep her mind off of things she couldn't do anything about. Yet, no matter how busy she was or how hard she tried to not think of Toby, she lost because she couldn't get him out of her mind. Whether she wanted to admit it or not, her head was always filled with thoughts of Toby. When she awoke in the morning, he was on her mind, and he was her last thought at night before she fell asleep. Plain and simple, Toby was in Jordan's mind all the time.

That Saturday morning in August, when her alarm clock sounded, she was grateful the rain had stopped and the sun was shining again. It had rained every day the past week and it would've been disappointing to start the choir anniversary celebration with rain, especially for the children as a number of their planned activities would be outside. Jordan arrived at church around ten o'clock that morning, the barbecue grill was up and going with slabs of ribs, chicken, hot dogs, hamburgers, and corn on the cob was wrapped in foil. One table was set up with plastic plates, colorful cups, utensils and napkins while other tables held everything from potato salad, pasta salad, macaroni and cheese, cold slaw, baked beans with bacon strips on top, collards, limas and rice. Another table held ice and soft drinks and still another table was laden with desserts.

It was fun watching the older members play bingo and board games while the kids rode their four-wheelers, played soft ball, participated in sack racing and other sports.

Around one o'clock, they broke from their activities, sat at rows of tables set up with colorful clothes and enjoyed lunch. At the conclusion of the afternoon activities, everything was returned to order, and they departed.

On Sunday, the anniversary program was inspirational. Plaques were given out to members for the work they had done in preparing for that day, and Jordan couldn't have beamed more with pride upon seeing the choir wearing their new robes.

School had only been in session a few weeks when Jordan already felt she needed a vacation. Not only were her students larger and a lot taller than her than in previous years, they were less interested in learning anything Jordan wanted to teach. And, as the school year progressed, things got progressively worse. Although Jordan had officially put her sorrows of the past and the worries about her future behind, she was determined to immerse herself completely in doing the best job she could in teaching the students who had a genuine interest in learning, find ways to connect with students who had no interest in school and find ways to pursue her heart's desire of fashion designing.

CHAPTER 15

Jordan entered the gymnasium for their Christmas party. The gym was decorated with numerous Christmas trees, lots of ornaments, red, white and green balloons and streamers were floating from the ceiling, and the floor was crowded with dancers.

Jordan wore a red silk off the shoulder, floor length gown with matching coat. Her grandmother's diamond necklace and earrings that were left to her went well with her outfit. The black leather stilettos and matching clutch purse completed her outfit. Her hair was piled high on top of her head with several curls cascading around her face and down her back, and her makeup was flawless. Jordan was a vision of beauty.

Maggie and Samantha rushed over to greet Jordan as she walked in. "Girl, you look fabulous," Samantha said, taking Jordan by her hand and twirling her around.

"Look at you. That outfit is hot."

"You ladies look great also," Jordan complimented.

"Where on earth did you find that outfit and don't tell us you made it. You paid a fortune for this little number," Maggie said.

"I made this outfit several weeks ago."

Maggie said, "This is lit. You look amazing."

"Thanks."

"Let's join the guys," Samantha said, linking her arm with Jordan's as the three ladies joined the men at the table where they chatted, had drinks and hors d'oeuvres and danced. Jordan couldn't help noticing Samantha and Maggie with their men and the stolen kisses they shared throughout the night. Although one handsome man was paying Jordan a lot of attention, she'd never felt more alone or missed Toby as much!

The party was festive and everyone was enjoying themselves, but Jordan was counting down to the hour when it would be a decent time to leave, and at ten and the party was starting to wind down, she said her goodbyes and left.

One Thursday afternoon in early January, it was raining and Jordan's mind was filled with thoughts of Toby. He was ever present in her mind. At the end of the school day, Jordan left the building and on her way to her car, she was grateful the rain had stopped especially since she'd forgotten her umbrella. She got into her car and headed home, but instead of turning on to the street that would take her home, she found herself going West on Interstate 20.

Halfway between Augusta and Atlanta, the rain returned. At first it was a drizzle but it quickly became a downpour. Jordan had wasted enough time and she didn't care whether it rained, sleet or snowed, she was going to Atlanta! She was going to see Toby! Today! She was going to let him know just how she felt, and she'd face whatever consequences there were. She had to see him! She had to! But, was it too late? Had she wasted too much time?!

Earlier, she'd secured Toby's office and home address. She was determined to go to Atlanta, find Toby and yes, she'd tell him she regret the unfortunate situation he found when he visited her but that she was there because she was in love with him, had been from the day they met, and she needed to see if there was anything left of what they'd discovered while in Montego Bay.

Hadn't Toby told her he was in love with her when they were in Jamaica and also in Augusta, when he came to see her? Was it possible that he could still be in love with her after what he found when he visited her?

Driving through the blinding rain, her only thought was to reach her destination. She checked the time on the dashboard clock. Three fifteen! She checked the address on a note pad lying on the seat next to her and entered the address into her GPS. It was getting dark, but she was almost there. It wasn't long before her GPS directed her to the Douglas Medical Center, where Toby's offices were located. After parking her car and shutting off the engine, Jordan got out of her car and raced towards the building. Completely soaked, she entered, brushed rain water from her face and hair, and she pulled off her coat to shake the rain from it.

She walked down the long tile corridor and stopped when she came upon the door with the name, Tobin Nathaniel Douglas, Oncologist, engraved in large gold plated letters. Jordan stood there hesitantly. She took a deep breath and wondered how Toby would receive her. Fuck that, she thought. I'm here now and I'll find out soon enough.

Jordan opened the door to the office and walked in, closing the door behind her. She walked up to the mahogany semi-circled desk where a beautiful, young Black woman looked up from her computer. She smiled and asked, "May I help you?"

Jordan pushed a piece of wet hair behind her ear. "Yes. Dr. Douglas, please?"

"Do you have an appointment, Ma'am?"

"No, no, I don't," Jordan stammered.

At that moment, the door to the inner office opened and an elderly Caucasian woman with warm grey eyes came out. She was followed by Toby with a file in his hand. He was smiling and talking with the older woman until he saw Jordan. Her eyes softened as she watched him approached the receptionist desk. That was the man she loved right there, she thought, and she wanted him and everyone else to know it.

Toby was shocked by the sight of Jordan standing in his office! Not only was she wet and looked cold, she also looked sensational. The woman was damn gorgeous. His heart took such a huge leap that he was certain she saw it thump through his medical coat. The image of Jordan only a few feet away caused a jolt that stirred in his groin, shaking him to his core and all he wanted to do was peel those soaked clothes off of her gorgeous body and make love to her passionately, intensely, and to not ever stop!

Toby shook his head to clear it of the thoughts he was harboring. With his patient he was now only inches away from Jordan. "Joycelyn, I'd like to see Mrs. Stewart in six months," he directed to the receptionist. He removed her heavy coat from the coat rack and helped her into it. "You get home safely, all right? It's nasty out there."

"Thank you, Dr. Douglas. My son should be here any minute now," she replied, eyes twinkling, and as she extended her small hand to his, a tall, slender man entered the office and approached them.

Toby and Mrs. Stewart's son shook hands, exchanged pleasantries and he embraced his mother. After saying goodbye, he escorted the elderly woman out. Toby turned his attention to Joycelyn and said, "I think this is it for today so why don't you get ready to go home. Have a good evening." He smiled politely at her.

"Okay, doctor. Have a good evening."

Toby turned to Jordan, took her by her arm and ushered her into his office. "What are you doing here, Jordan?" He took her coat from her arm, hung it over the back of a chair, and he pulled a clean handkerchief from his pocket. He wiped her face and hair dry. He walked away from her to adjust the thermostat on the wall. Then, he went behind his desk and pulled a freshly laundered shirt from a drawer. "You didn't answer my question. Why are you here?" He asked, walking back over to her, pulling the wet burgundy turtleneck sweater over her head and threw it on a chair.

"I came to see you!"

"Why do you want to see me? Are you ill?!" He unbuttoned the shirt, put it on Jordan and buttoned it from the neck all the way down.

She was shaking but looked defiantly into his eyes. "No, I'm not ill." Her body was cold and shaking but she looked defiantly into his eyes.

"You're a long way from home, aren't you?"

"That's not important."

"I still don't understand why you came here to see me?"

"I came here to see you and...and," she stuttered, "and to tell you that I love you, Toby. I am in love with you."

"Oh really?!" His own tone matched her defiance.

"Yes!"

"I find that hard to believe."

He could be as stubborn as he wanted to be, she thought but that wasn't going to stop her. She was there for one reason and she was going to see it through.

"I've always known that I love you, Toby. From the day we met, even before you told me you loved me, and I've thought about you every day since that time. I see your face before I open my eyes in the morning. Every morning! And, it hurts like hell when I think of living my life without you in it. I love you. Isn't that enough?"

"Some would say that sometime love is *not* enough," he said, coolly not letting Jordan know that her words caused a jolt of electricity to ripple through his body with such force that it made him weak, almost speechless. She had no idea how long he'd wanted to hear her say those words.

"Yes, some would say that, but what about you, Toby?" She looked up into his eyes. "What do you say? Is love enough for you?"

"Maybe!"

Have I waited too long, she wondered, suddenly feeling sad. Very sad!

"Did I make a mistake coming here?"

"What about what's his name?"

"There is no one else." She looked honestly into his eyes. "It was a terrible mistake, allowing Frank back into my home. I don't expect you to understand. Honestly, I don't understand it either. I'm not making excuses for what I did. All I can say is that I was very lonely. It was stupid, impulsive, but the most painful thing was that I thought I'd never see you again. I felt I'd lost you forever and then,,," she stopped herself for a moment and took a deep breath before continuing, "and then a really good friend suddenly died. It was just a lot to handle."

"So you decided to sleep with that moron again after declaring you were through with him? What do you expect me to say? What do you want from me?" His eyes pierced into hers.

"I don't know what I want from you. Maybe I just want you to know that I love you, and I want you to love me back. Can you do that or is that too much to ask?"

"We'll talk about it. Right now, I'm taking you home, get you out of those wet clothes and into a nice warm bath. Are you up for that?"

"Yes," was all Jordan could say. The fact that he didn't turn her away and send her back to Augusta was more than enough for now.

Toby removed his medical coat, put on the jacket to complete his Brooks Brothers suit and pulled his heavy coat from a hook behind his office door. He walked back over to Jordan and helped her into his coat that landed near her ankles.

"I can't wear your coat. What are you gonna wear? It's freezing outside." Her face was etched with concern.

"I'll be fine. I don't want you to get soaked again tonight." He finished buttoning up his coat on her and looked down at her. "Ready?"

"Yes."

Toby readjusted the thermostat. He pulled a huge umbrella from where it was standing in a trash can. He shut off the lights, escorted Jordan out of his office and after locking up, he opened the umbrella, pulled Jordan close to himself, and they rushed to his car, parked several spaces from hers.

"What about my car?" she asked.

"It'll be fine. We'll get it tomorrow."

"Who said I'm spending the night?"

"I know you're not leaving here in this weather tonight." He was certain of that.

156

They got into Toby's sleek navy late model Jaguar and he started it up. "It'll be warm in here pretty soon."

"That's fine." Her teeth were chattering. Suddenly she asked, "Do you still love me?"

He didn't answer but a smile touched his lips as he looked over at her before backing out of the parking space. It was one of those times when she knew that sometimes a lot can be said without a word being spoken.

They rode in silence through the busy, wet streets before Toby spoke. "I'm sorry to hear you lost a friend." He glanced at her before returning his attention back to the highway. "Were the two of you close?"

"Yes. I knew her all my life."

"You don't mean Mrs. Irene?"

Jordan looked over at him, surprised he remembered her talking about Mrs. Irene. "Yes. She was like a mother to my siblings and I. When she died, we were devastated."

"I'm sure." He glanced at her again. "I'm sorry."

They fell silent again.

After a while, Jordan turned and looked at Toby. He noticed and asked, "What's going on?"

"Your assistant is gorgeous." Jordan tried to sound nonchalant.

He smirked. "I've noticed."

"I'm sure you have," Jordan nearly snapped at him.

He was taken aback. "Are you jealous?"

"No." She looked away. "I was simply making an observation."

"Okay." Toby continued to smile.

They merged with the traffic, heading South on Interstate 85. Then as though each willed the song to play, "Am I Dreaming," began to pour out of the radio speakers. Toby and Jordan were so happy to be together that they felt they were in the middle of a beautiful dream.

He reached over, took Jordan's small cold hand into his and after massaging it a while, he squeezed it, then he held it.

Within a half hour, they pulled into the driveway of a huge house in an upscale neighborhood in Atlanta. He didn't release her hand until he pulled into the garage.

"By the way, Joycelyn is married to a very nice man whom she loves very much, and they have three beautiful kids," he said grinning as he got out of the car and walked around to open the door for her.

Great, Jordan thought happily.

"So this is where you live?" She was thinking that was a lot of house for one person, and the grounds were beautiful.

"Yes."

"It certainly is huge."

"I bought this place after my mother became ill. I didn't want her living alone and she didn't want to live with me, but I insisted. If she needed her space, the house is large enough that we wouldn't bump into each other. She was going through so much and I wanted her with me."

"I understand. I would have done the same."

"I know." Toby had learned a lot about Jordan on the day they met, and he believed her.

CHAPTER 16

Entering Toby's home, Jordan felt as though she'd landed onto the pages of a luxury homes and gardens magazine. It was exquisite. No other word for it. After living in the house with her brother, Stevie and visiting Frank's home, Jordan wasn't sure men were capable of occupying orderly surroundings. She could see that Toby was an exception. Everything about the property was exceptional, even the gardens. And although it was January, there were winter flowers in bloom allowing for a most picturesque view.

The house was modern and spacious with an open floor plan allowing her to see from the front door to the wall of windows and French doors at the back of the house. The ceilings were high and the floors, highly polished. Everything in its perfect place and although it hinted of masculinity, there was also a simple elegance displayed among the white leather couches, rich brown oak tables, huge potted plants, modern pieces of art adorning the walls, and expensive area rugs on the floors. The kitchen featured stainless steel appliances and granite counter tops. Toby and Jordan walked down the huge foyer and up the stairs together. He led her down a long hall and through a huge master bedroom dominated by an equally huge bed covered in chocolate and beige satin comforter with matching pillows and a chocolate dust ruffle. The huge double-glazed windows were without curtains but covered with alabaster wooden shutters. Jordan could see the massive bathroom through the open door.

She glanced around. There were numerous photographs of a gorgeous woman on tables and above the fireplace. Some of the pictures had the same woman, either holding Toby on her lap when he was a toddler or where he was standing beside a chair where the woman sat. Toby's mother, Jordan thought. They shared similar features.

Jordan didn't mention the photographs, but she said, "Beautiful home."

"Thank you. I'll show you around later."

"Okay."

They walked together into the bathroom. Toby turned on the water in the bathtub, pulled some towels from the linen closet and placed them on the sink.

He was about to leave Jordan to take a bath when she said, "There's only one problem."

He turned to look at her. "What's that?"

"I didn't bring any clothes."

"That's okay. I've got plenty," Toby said, a sly smile passed across his face. "You've worn my clothes before."

She gave him a smile as he left the room.

He looks good, she thought. Damn good! Toby was a handsome man. Right now he looked even better than he did the last time she saw him. Toby returned soon carrying a pair of his pajamas, handing them to Jordan.

"You want me to help you with that bath?" He gave her another sly smile.

"I suppose I can manage from here." She returned the same sly smile. She closed the door after him.

While Jordan bathe, Toby took a shower before going into the kitchen. He filled the kettle with water, placed it on the stove and he began preparing dinner. When Jordan entered the kitchen, her hair up in a pony tail and wearing Toby's pajamas, she saw that he'd changed into casual clothes, he was setting plates of toast, bacon and eggs on the table and humming a popular tune. He stopped and his entire face lit up at seeing her. His eyes sparkled and his mouth widened into a breathtaking smile as Jordan approached him. He picked up several hangers from the island that held Jordan's sweater, slacks and coat. "I'm just gonna hang these up to dry. Have a seat. I'll be right back and we can have something to eat." He went off to the bathroom and returned within minutes.

Jordan got up from the table. "Where are your cups and saucers?" She asked.

"Over the sink." He removed a jar of jam and a dish of cantaloupe from the refrigerator and placed them on the table. "I'm a breakfast kind of guy. I could have breakfast three times a day."

"A man after my own heart. Breakfast is my favorite meal also."

Jordan set the cups and saucers on the table and brought over a pot of heated water. She picked up a box of tea from the island and after filling each cup with hot water, they sat at the table. She said, "About the last time that we saw each other."

Toby interrupted her, "Are you finished with that joker?"

"Yes. That very night, and I'm done."

"Then," he said, looking into her eyes, "we don't need to talk about it anymore."

Jordan was surprised by his response, and she saw the same intense blazing heat in his eyes that burned in her own heart. She reached across the table and took his hands into hers and after the blessing, he held onto one of her hands as they began to have their first meal together in the United States.

"How do you feel?" Toby asked, forking eggs into his mouth.

"Great. That hot bath was what I needed. Thank you." She tried to pull her hand from his grasp only to have him tighten his hold. "I just want to put some honey in my tea. Would you like some?"

"Yes, please," he said, releasing her hand, but not wanting to. Jordan was sitting across the table from him, in his home having dinner. Toby could never remember being so happy. He asked, "So how was Christmas?"

"Nothing special! The twins and I had breakfast at my house and exchanged gifts. Late afternoon, they joined friends, and I spent some time sewing and watching movies. That's about it." Jordan poured honey into his cup. "Say when."

"When."

"So, how did you spend Christmas?"

"I slept in until early afternoon, I had a few people over for drinks and later some of us hit a couple parties. That was about it."

"I bought you something for Christmas." She added honey to her tea cup.

His eyes lit up. "You bought me a gift?"

"Yes I did."

"I've got to do something about that because I didn't get you anything."

"That's not necessary. I got something I thought you might like."

"What is it?"

"I'm not telling you," Jordan answered, chomping on a piece of toast before sipping her tea. Toby reached across the table for her hand again.

"Where is it? Do I have to go with you to Augusta to get it?" He asked.

"If I said yes, would you do it?"

"Of course I would. Why? Were you thinking that I wouldn't?"

"I wasn't sure." Then, after a moment's pause, Jordan asked, "Why didn't you contact me?"

He blinked and looked at her. Her question had caught him by surprise. "You sent me away. Did you expect me to?"

"I'd hoped you would."

"Why didn't you contact me?"

"I wasn't sure you wanted to hear from me."

"Of course I did, but I ain't gonna lie," he took a deep breath before continuing, "you really pissed me off when you told me you were getting back with that cheating, no good son of a bitch so I felt then that it was over between us. You seemed so definite. At least that was what I thought at the time. I should have stayed and handled things differently. I know that now. That was my mistake. I knew you weren't completely at fault. I admit, I didn't handle things well, and I regret that." He stared at her. "The feelings I have for you are strong. So, tell me, what are we gonna do about that?"

"What do you mean?" Jordan's fork of eggs stopped midway before reaching her mouth. She was surprised by his question and her forked hovered in the air briefly.

Toby sat back in his chair. "I've achieved much of the things I've wanted to do in my life except one of the most important things. For a long time I've wanted to fall in love, get married and have a family. Well, I have fallen in love, now I want to fulfill the rest of my dream."

She placed her cup in the saucer. "What

Are you saying? Are you saying you forgive me?"

He gave her a mischievous grim. "No, you're not gonna get off that easy. You're gonna pay for what you did."

His smile told her he was teasing. She smiled at him, got up and cleared the table, putting the dishes into the dishwasher. He got up, pulled a bottle of wine from the refrigerator and glasses from the cabinet and filled each glass. "Can I make a toast?!"

"Of course. What are we toasting to?"

"To us being together. Our future."

"Can you envision a future with me?"

"Sure I can. Can you envision your future without me?"

Jordan tilted her head to the side and smiled sweetly at him. "No. No, I can't. There's nothing I want more than to spend my life with you, but are you sure that's what you want?"

"I'm sure."

Jordan sighed happily, looking into his eyes. They clicked their glasses together and sipped their wine.

"You know I'm thinking about giving up teaching at the end of the school year and moving to New York or here to give fashion designing a try."

"Would that make you happy?"

"That's a part of what would make me happy."

"What is the other part?" He asked.

"You, Toby. You."

They got out of their chairs and instantly, they were in each other's arms, their bodies melding together. She felt herself gasp as their mouths collided like magnets. The first touch of her lips sent sparks of electricity through him. He heard her small sob and tasted her salty tears. He pulled away to ask, "Why are you crying, baby?"

"I'm happy, Toby. I'm so happy to be here with you." Unblinkingly, she met his gaze, wanting him to kiss her again as he'd just done. Jordan couldn't understand why Toby was willing to forgive her so easily but she happy with his decision.

His gaze was intense, mesmerizing. She stood still in his arms, her heart racing as she anticipated the soft touch of his lips as they reclaimed hers. As he increased the pressure of his lips against hers, she heard the quickening of his breath and felt the pounding of his heart. She kissed him back with all the passion she possessed, Toby! Toby! Toby! His name floated around inside her head.

When the kiss ended, they gazed into each other's lush filled eyes. After a moment, he said, "Here we are."

"Here we are," she echoed, feeling his male hardness pressing hard against her.

"You do things to me, lady," he whispered against her ear.

She rubbed her hands over his chest in a gentle caress. His hands came up to her breasts and using his thumbs, he teased her nipples that were hard and erect. He kissed her again and a soft moan escaped from her.

Toby snatched his mouth from hers, ripped open the front of the pajama top she was wearing exposing her creamy, ripened breasts and immediately his mouth went to her erect buds greeting him. He went from one nipple to the next, licking, sucking, lashing with his tongue until Jordan was delirious with passion.

Toby's lips trailed from her breasts up her neck then back to reclaim her mouth and then their tongues dueled tirelessly. Then, effortlessly, he picked her up, she wrapped her arms around his neck, snuggled in his arm and resting her head against his chest as he carried her to his bedroom. They fell onto his California King bed. He kicked off his shoes, removed Jordan's pajama top and pushed the pajama bottom down her curvy voluptuous hips, her legs, and off her feet.

Toby was mesmerized by the sight of her nude body lying on the comforter. She watched him breathlessly with anticipation as he unbuttoned his shirt, tossed it aside and kicked out of his pants. She not only noticed he wasn't wearing underwear, but she couldn't miss his huge gorgeous member. How could she not notice it? It stood hard and erect in front of him. Yes! Long! Thick! Gorgeous! She took in a sharp intake of air. She sent up a big Thank You to the Almighty. All she could think about was how much she wanted him to plant himself inside her wet, molten core.

He stretched alongside her, and for a moment, they gazed at each other. Just as Jordan couldn't believe she was in bed naked next to him, neither could he. She went eagerly and willingly into his arms as he reached for her.

As his fingers moved over her satin aroused body, heat that matched hers exactly burst through him. Every where he touched her, his hands sent spurts of fire throughout her body and she began to squirm under his touch. His lips brushed across hers.

"I can't believe you're actually here and in my arms," he said in a low, husky voice. He stared down at her lips and then slowly, ever so slowly, his fingers traced down the smooth naked skin of her abdomen, down to her greatest secret of all. She parted her legs for him, welcoming him to caress her there.

He obeyed her silent request touching her there, feeling her slickness, he stroked her gently and as his lips returned to hers, more friction ensued. His tongue nudged the tip of hers causing the core deep inside her to explode and shower her body with sparks of sensation. Their kiss was soft, demanding, gentle yet passionate.

He saw the burning desire in her eyes that equaled the smoldering coal of his own need. As he wrapped his lips around one nipple and sucked hard on it, his finger tips did other amazing things to the other. His mouth descended down her body to her navel, on to her womanly mound. Ever so slowly, he used his tongue to penetrate her and dwelled there, for a while.

When Toby came up to face her again, she reached down between his legs, and finding what she sought, she wrapped her fingers around him, stroking his hardened, healthy member vigorously before guiding him to her eagerly awaiting cavity. He slammed into her with such force, it took her breath away. Once inside her, he stayed there, loving the feel of her delicate flesh swaddling him, her tight, biting flesh surrounding his male hardness and choking him. Now, with the drive of a well oil machine, he withdrew slightly before slamming into her over and over again, fast and fierce until he thought he would surely lose his mind.

She wrapped her legs around his hips, clamping his body to hers and answered his deep, powerful thrusts with her own total reckless abandonment. Without withdrawing he rolled over, pulling her on top of him. She pulled her knees up against his waist and moved her hips fiercely against him, meeting his hips and as he slammed his body upward into her, she rode him like a strong, proud, powerful animal.

Back on top now, as she sucked his tongue frantically, sending spurts of undeniable pleasure coursing through his body, he plunged into her hard and fast, at super human velocity. Then, with one final thrust, together they experienced the most magnificent climax. And, still in bed, joined as one, their sweat was a common pool.

CHAPTER 17

Later, as Jordan and Toby lay in bed, for the first time in her life, she felt wrapped in an island of insanity and an ocean of security, all at the same time. Jordan didn't know when she'd ever felt as complete, if she ever had, and she loved that feeling.

Toby looked at her. "When I thought I'd lost you, I wasn't sure what I was going to do with the rest of my life."

"I'm sorry."

"Yes! I fell in love with you so quickly, so completely, I knew it had to be real. I'd never experienced anything resembling those feelings and when you sent me away, it threw my whole world into chaos. I didn't know how to handle it. I've never been involved in a situation where I didn't know what my next move would be. Never! This was new territory for me. So, there I was floundering, wondering whether you were real or just a figment of my imagination.

You probably wonder now why I got over so quickly what happened when I visited you months ago."

"Yes."

"Jordan, I know what I want. I know you and I believe that you want me. If this is what we both want, why play games? Why waste time, dragging this out and bringing a lot of unhappiness to both of us. We're not kids." He paused before taking a deep breath. "Life is short and can be cruel, but it can also be terrific. You just have to believe it in your heart and your soul, otherwise what's the use. I want you. I need you, and I want you and me to live our best lives from now on together." He paused again. "When I look at you now, touch you, I know you are real. You are that woman I met in Jamaica. When I'm with you, I know who I am and where I'm going. You're all that I want and I want you to always be with me. Does that make sense?"

"Perfect sense," she replied, softly. Her heart thumped with emotion. She'd never felt more joy than at that moment. She moved deeper into his arms.

Sometime later when they released each other, she said, "I had no intentions of spending the night."

"No?"

"No! I intended to come here, tell you I'm in love with you, ask for forgiveness for my stupidity and leave, hoping you'd give us a chance to see where we can take this."

"So I foiled your plans, huh?" he said, running his nose against her hair. "What would you say if I asked you to stay on here with me?" The room suddenly became very quiet, still. "Hello," he said with laughter in his voice, "is anyone there?"

"What do you mean? You can't mean what I think. I want us to be together but…"

"Now, how did I know there was going to be a "but" in there somewhere?"

"I was going to say but I don't want to rush things. I'd like us to get to know each other better. Don't you?!"

"Jordan, the one sure thing that life has taught me is to not put off anything that I want. Go after it. Hell, take the risk."

"Toby, I've got a job, I've got a house. You know I can't move here now. Please tell me you're joking."

Toby asked, "You can't or you won't?"

"That's not fair."

"Why waste more time? You have to start living for yourself. When are you going to do something for you?"

She grinned. "I just did something for myself."

"No baby, that was for me."

She looked at him and they burst out laughing.

"This year. As soon as this school year is over," she said and that was when she knew for sure that this would be her final year teaching ninth grade Math. She would give designing a try and if it didn't work out, she'd deal with it then, but for now, she knew exactly what she wanted to do.

Toby sat up in bed. "Are you serious? Are you really gonna move in with me?"

"I don't know whether I'll be moving in with you, but I'm certain I'll be leaving Augusta in the next few months."

"And you will be coming to Atlanta."

"Yeah, I believe so."

"In a few months, huh?"

"Do you have a problem with that?"

"Hell no. If I had it my way, I'd keep you here with me, but I know you've got things to do so that you can move forward with a whole new venture."

Could this man be real? She thought. Could anyone be this special? "I love you, Toby," she cooed.

"I love you, baby."

"Thank you for seeing me today."

"Thank you for coming to me today."

Jordan reached for Toby. They ended up wrapped in each other's arms, kissing passionately and making love. He slammed into her with a fierceness that she had never experienced before, and she wanted it to go on forever. Longer—if possible!

Jordan and Toby sat at the kitchen table enjoying a late night snack she had prepared.

"This is good," Toby complimented, munching on tuna salad on a cracker.

"Honey, it's just tuna." Jordan sipped her hot chocolate.

"Yeah, I know but what the heck did you do to it?"

"I just added a boiled egg, a little salad dressing, sweet cube pickles and a dash of seasoned salt and pepper."

"Well, I love it." He picked up a knife, spread more of the tuna salad onto a cracker and put it to Jordan's lips. She took a bite from it and he devoured the remainder. "When we are done here, let me show you around. You must think I'm a terrible host."

"I think you're an excellent host, and I'd love to see the rest of your home."

"We're going to get you some clothes tomorrow."

"I don't need any clothes. My own clothes will be dried by morning and I can wear them home."

"You don't think I'm gonna let you leave me tomorrow, do you?"

"Yes. I've done what I came here to do, so I'll go back home get my lesson plan and everything done for work on Monday."

"What's wrong with spending a little extra time with me and leave Sunday. Besides, I want to take you out for a nice dinner, then later we can dance a little, the way we did in Montego Bay. You remember that, don't you?" He finished his hot chocolate.

"Yes," she breathed. "I'll never forget the day that led into that awesome night." Then she whispered, "A day in paradise."

"What was that?"

"Oh, nothing."

They shared a silent look and a loving smile.

Toby and Jordan got up from the table and walked first through the downstairs portion of the house where there was a library that doubled as an office, a home theater, two bedrooms, a huge walk-in closet with an island and hardwood shelves on the walls, and a billiard room. On the other side of the house beyond the kitchen was a breakfast room, formal dining room, two bathrooms, and a gym. They went upstairs, each room more spectacular than the previous one. There were three bedrooms with accompanying balconies to each room, overlooking the glass enclosed backyard pool surrounded by chairs, tables, books and a large screen TV for his indoor pleasures, winter or summer. One bedroom was a master suite that included double sinks and a garden tub. There was also a powder room and lots of closet space. The furniture, a combination of modern and antique and she smiled at someone's good taste.

They returned to the bedroom. As soon as they were settled in each other's arms, Jordan sneezed.

Toby sat up in bed. "Are you alright?" He inquired.

She sneezed again and again. "I'm not sure." She pulled tissues from a box on the nightstand and dabbed her nose. "My throat is a little scratchy."

"I've got something in the medicine cabinet that I can give you. Lie down, I'll be right back."

Toby got out of bed. He fluffed Jordan's pillows, pulled the covers up on her and left the room. He returned shortly with a cup of hot tea, a couple of cold tablets and a bottle of water, that he handed her.

"Take these, baby," he said, and she obeyed.

She took a sip of water to swallow the pills. "Thank you," she said and sipped her tea.

Toby sat on the side of the bed until Jordan finished her tea. He took the cup to the kitchen, returned to the room and he climbed into bed beside her. Not long afterward he heard her soft, even breathing and knew she'd fallen asleep.

Jordan's sleep was restless. She tossed and turned, rolling over in bed. Her hand grazed Toby's chest, then covered his nipple. The touch sent shock waves through him. The sweet fragrance of her body drifted to him and the fire in his vein began to ignite. He watched Jordan most of the night, as she slept. It didn't matter what happened with her before that moment. All he knew then was that he loved her, he always would, and he wanted to take care of her. As she slept, Toby lifted her hand from his chest and gently massaged it. He ran her hand along the side of his face, he kissed her palm and then, he placed her hand by her side and pulled up the covers.

The next morning, Jordan woke late with a temperature, puffy eyes and a headache but a vivid memory of the evening before she got sick. The night had been a dream come true! Literally!

Toby called in a prescription that he picked up from a nearby pharmacy. When he returned, Jordan climbed out of bed, took a shower and slipped into a clean pair of his pajamas. He was able to get her to eat a pieces of toast, more hot tea, and she took her first dose of medication before going back to bed.

While Jordan rested, Toby found things to do to keep busy, including watering the plant that was given to him when his mother passed away. Later that afternoon when Jordan got out of bed, she found Toby in the kitchen putting away groceries. A copy of the Atlanta Constitutional Journal lay on the table.

"I thought I heard voices," Jordan said.

"Art, a buddy of mine, was here. I asked him to drop off your car."

"You think of everything. Thank you." She walked over and gave him a hug.

"Looks like you're feeling better."

"As good as new," she smiled up at him.

Then they sat down to eat. Toby was pleased that Jordan's appetite had returned. She ate a bowl of chicken noodle soup, some saltine crackers, and she drank a large glass of orange juice, while he finished the leftover tuna salad.

It rained all day; Jordan and Toby snuggled on the couch in the den and talked as they watched the rain and laughed, pretending to count the drops as they fell from the sky, forming puddles beyond the indoor pool.

"Sixty, sixty-one, sixty-two," Toby counted, chuckling.

"Eighty-six, eighty-seven," Jordan raced along, laughing as they teased each other.

That went on for a little while. Then, late afternoon, they watched a movie, talked and played Scrabble, their favorite game.

Toby had started dinner, Jordan insisted on helping. It was a simple meal of broiled steaks, baby potatoes, sweet peas and rolls. They had cheesecake for dessert.

That night in bed, Toby pulled Jordan close to him. Having her body next to him caused his member to come to life like a runaway train and as much as he wanted her, he kissed her lightly on her lips and held her in his arms all night.

Jordan was awakened Sunday morning to the smell of coffee. She opened her eyes to see Toby smiling as he approached her carrying a breakfast tray. "How are you feeling this morning?" He asked.

"I'm good. How are you doing?"

Jordan had noticed sadness in Toby's eyes from the time she arrived. She wished she could erase it only she wasn't sure how. She wanted to ask him why he appeared so sad but refrained because she felt that sadness was brought on by her own actions.

"What have you got there?" She asked.

Toby put the tray on the night table and sat on the side of the bed. He felt Jordan's forehead and her temperature was back. "Are you feeling okay?"

"Better than yesterday. The food smells good."

Toby had prepared grits, scrambled eggs, turkey bacon, juice and coffee.

"Is this okay with you or would you like something else?"

"I'll eat some of what you have here." She gave him a weak smile as she sat up in bed. Toby set the tray in her lap. "No one has ever served me breakfast in bed before."

"Never?!"

"Never! This is a first."

"Well, I intend to give you lots of firsts."

She smiled at him. Then, she bit off a piece of bacon.

Toby ate a full breakfast. Jordan ate enough so that she could take her meds.

"Breakfast was great," she complimented.

Throughout the day, Toby fed Jordan what she felt she could eat; either toast, soup, lots of orange juice, green tea with honey and lemon.

Late Sunday afternoon, although Jordan was feeling much better, Toby announced, "I'm calling in sick for you tomorrow. I don't want you out there facing this crazy Atlanta Sunday afternoon traffic. You're going to stay here and let me take care of you. Besides, I could use a few days myself."

"You can't take off from work to take care of me."

"Of course I can. I'll check in but it'll be fine. We don't usually schedule much for Monday or Tuesday. There're doctors on call so there won't be any problems. Besides I haven't taken a day off since I went to Jamaica, so I think I am entitled to a day or two."

"You don't need to do that. I'm fine."

"I'm sure, but I've made the decision and I'll call and put everything in place."

"Honey, are you sure?"

"I love it when you call me honey." He smiled then added, "I haven't told you but Friday night was amazing."

She felt herself blush, redness rose in her cheeks. She said, "It was for me as well."

"I'm sorry I didn't get the chance to take you out and treat you to a nice dinner and a night of slow, sexy dancing."

"You've been great." She smiled and added, "I never get sick. I can't believe I waited until I got here to get sick."

"You've never had anyone to take care of you before."

Jordan smiled. "You think that's it?"

He smiled back. "I'm certain. Kiss me."

"No baby. I could make you sick."

Toby rolled his head to one side and said, "I'd definitely get sick if you *don't* kiss me."

Early Monday morning, Toby called Cherokee High School. He informed the secretary that Jordan was sick and wouldn't be at work for a couple of days. Then he called his office, told his staff he was taking off a few days and would be in touch.

On Tuesday afternoon, though Jordan felt she'd completely recovered, she placed a call to the principal and informed them that she'd be out the rest of the week. When she informed Toby, he was surprised and ecstatic with the good news.

"That's great. This will give me an opportunity to cook for you."

"You have cooked for me."

"I want to cook you a real meal."

"So you cook like that?

"Yeah girl, I can burn."

"Look at you; you are a successful oncologist, you showed me some of your paintings last night, which are absolutely fabulous and now you're telling me you cook."

"Yes, I really do."

"My man. A real renaissance man."

"I like the sound of that. The, 'my man,' part."

They burst into laughter.

The following afternoon, Toby took Jordan to the aquarium and later, shopping. He wanted to splurge on her but she insisted on getting only two pairs of jeans, two crop neck sweaters, and he insisted she get something for herself but would benefit him more.

A couple of hours later, carrying packages and chuckling about a bad joke Toby told her, they returned to his house to the smell of her spaghetti sauce that she had left on low on the stove earlier.

Toby took their coats and the packages and put them away. He took Jordan's hand and led her into the kitchen. He pulled a bottle of wine from the refrigerator and filled two glasses that they took with them to the den.

"I wish you would've allowed me to buy you that cute little red number that we saw in that lingerie shop. I would've love seeing that body of yours in that. Uh, uh, uh." He gave her that sly smile she loved so much.

Shaking her head and returning a sly smile of her own, she said, "Yeah?!"

"Oh yeah! I'm happy that you did allow me to get one lingerie set," he said, then more softly against her ear, he added, "and I can assure you that when you put it on, you won't be wearing it very long."

"No?!"

"No!"

"I thought you wanted to see it on me."

"That's why you won't be wearing it long because once I see you in it, I'm gonna bite it right off of you."

"You're so bad."

"Yeah, I know."

"You're admitting it?"

"I am."

They looked at each other and they burst out laughing.

"You're too much."

"I'll take that too," he said, chuckling and she joined in.

Jordan set her wine glass on the coffee table and got up from the couch. Toby caught her hand and asked, "Where are you going?"

"I want to check the sauce and put the spaghetti on. You wanna come?"

"I sure do wanna cum."

When he laughed, she knew exactly why. She swatted his arm. "Bad, bad, bad."

Arm around her waist, they went to the kitchen together. She picked up the wooden spoon from the stove, stirred the sauce and dipped a spoonful from the pot. After cooling it with her breath, she said, "Taste this and tell me what you think."

She watched him, her eyes bright with anticipation as he tasted the sauce.

"Umm. Delicious." He licked his lips.

"You will be doing this tomorrow."

"Doing what?"

"You told me you're gonna cook dinner for me?"

"Yes."

"Then you can do it tomorrow."

Toby took the spoon from Jordan's hand, pulled her into his arms and kissed her. She stabbed her tongue deep into his mouth. As their kiss accelerated, he removed her clothes as she did his. He wanted her so bad. He lifted her up on the counter and they continued kissing. Then her phone rang. They ignored the persistent ring as long as they could before she groaned and pulled away saying, "I'd better get that. It's probably one of my siblings."

Toby moved away from her, picked up her phone from the table and handed it to her. She moved closer to Toby, placed an arm around his neck and drew him to her.

"Stevie, what's going on?" She asked and listened. "What? Frank? He did what?" Jordan twisted her ear lobe. "I'm out of town, but I'll be home in a couple of hours. I'll call you from the road."

Toby leaned away from Jordan, looking at her, concern all over his face. "What's going on?"

"I've gotta go. I'm sorry but I've gotta get home," she said, hurriedly leaving the kitchen, heading toward the bedroom.

"Talk to me. What's wrong?" He asked, following behind her.

"I'm going home," she said, putting her things together.

"Can I drive you home? Or would you like me to fly to Augusta with you?"

"No, this is something I've gotta handle myself."

"You're upset, and I don't want you driving in your condition. Please let me help."

"Honey, I'm fine, I promise you. I'm gonna drive home, but I'll call you."

Without further explanation, Jordan quickly got dressed. Toby picked up her packages from the floor, he walked her out and placed the packages in the back seat. She kissed him briefly on the lips, got into her car and drove away as he watched her, sadly. Soon, Jordan was on the Interstate, heading home and to the trouble that awaited her.

CHAPTER 18

Speeding down the highway heading East on I-26, Jordan called her brother. When he answered, she said, "Okay Stevie, run this whole thing by me again. How in the hell could something like this happened? What the fuck is going on with your sister?" After several questions flew out of Jordan's mouth, she stopped talking and listened to Stevie. "It was Frank who got Steffie involved in his mess? Selling drugs, Stevie?" Jordan asked and listened some more. "So this is how you two are able to afford such an expensive house? This is how you two are paying the bills, Steven Alexander Banks?!" Stevie tried to answer her question, but she interrupted, "You had to know this was going on. Not much gets by you and you know I know that. How long has this been going on anyway?" She asked and said as if in a whisper to herself, "Steffie's been selling drugs for Frank!"

"Seven or eight months, and Steffie is away from home a lot more."

"What do you think that means? Does she have a new boyfriend? I know she's been dating but I didn't think it was serious. Talk to me, Stevie. I can't figure out what's going on with her."

"Honestly I don't know, but if it is what I think it is, then somebody's gonna answer to me," Stevie said, and Jordan could hear anger in his voice. Rage!

Stevie had always been very protective of his sisters, especially his twin.

"What are you talking about?"

"You know I don't like to say anything about any situation until I know the facts. Right now, I'm gathering facts. By the way, you haven't been home for a few days. Where have you been? Are you okay?"

"Yeah, I was visiting a friend in Atlanta."

"I hope you enjoyed your time there. Glad to see you doing something for yourself. You should do more of that."

Jordan checked her watch.

"I should be there in about an hour. Meet me at my house."

"You be safe out there."

When Jordan hung up from her brother, she called Toby.

"What's going on, Jordan?" He asked and she knew he had questions about why she didn't tell him anything before she left.

"Honey, I'm sorry for leaving that way but it looks like Steffie has gotten herself into something terrible."

"What does Frank have to do with it?" Toby demanded. When Jordan shared with him everything Stevie told her, he said, "I'm coming."

"No, I don't want you to do that, but thank you. I'll get back with you," she said, then she added, "and Toby, I appreciate you so much, and I love you."

"You sure you don't want me to come?"

"I'm sure."

"I love you, but I don't like that you won't allow me to get involved with something that concerns you and your family. I don't have a good feeling about that Frank dude."

"He is a messy character, but I need you to trust me on this. If I need you, I promise, I'll be in touch."

At a quarter to nine, Jordan pulled into her driveway and parked her car next to Stevie's. The lights were on inside her house. She got out of her car, walked up to the front door, and Stevie opened it for her. He kissed her on her cheek.

"Where is Steffie? What else have you learned?" She asked, breathlessly.

Just then, there were sounds coming from the hall bathroom. They turned to see Steffie coming out, looking like hell warmed over. Jordan knew Steffie had some reservations about them seeing her after her secret had been exposed, but Steffie looked petrified, and Jordan or Steven couldn't help but wonder what was causing her such panic. They hadn't seen her that frightened in a long time, a very long time!

Jordan dropped her purse and shopping bags on a table. "What's going on with you, Missy?" Jordan stood with one hand on her akimbo and the other on the table.

"Hey Jordan." Steffie kissed her sister on the cheek, walked over to the couch and dropped down hard on it.

"What are you doing selling drugs for Frank? Hell, selling drugs period?" Jordan demanded to know.

"I know I've disappointed both of you, and I'm sorry," Steffie began dropping her face in both hands. When she raised her head again, looking at her siblings, she continued, "You know we've never had

194

much and you know how I've always liked nice things." She shrugged. "Well this was a quicker and easier way of getting the things that I wanted."

Jordan exploded. "What the fuck are you thinking, Steffie? Listen to what you're saying. Do you know how you sound?" Steffie opened her mouth to speak but Jordan lashed out at her again. "Why do you think we've worked so hard to get you a good education? We did it so you can get a good job, be financially stable and get the things you want the right way? And, why in hell do you think you need to get mixed up with a goddamn drug dealer and the likes of that dumb ass, crazy ass Frank? Do you have any idea what you're doing?"

"Not exactly."

"Not exactly?" She tugged her ear lobe.

"I thought I did."

Steffie looked more confused than ever. Stevie went over and took a seat next to her.

Jordan asked. "Then tell me how does this work? How do you get involved with something when you don't understand all the ins and outs of what it is that you're supposed to be doing?"

Steffie didn't comment. She still had a look of confusion on her face. Stevie patted her hand.

"How did you know that Frank is involved with selling drugs?" Stevie asked.

"He told me. Well, he didn't at first. He didn't tell me he was dealing drugs but his actions said it all. I was at his club several times and I couldn't help noticing who was in the mix and the ones who were just partygoer as my friends and I were."

"How did he approach you?"

"One night, some friends and I were at a club. Frank was there, looking real flashy; nice threads, expensive watch. You know. He was with a group of people, all dressed really nice. They all came in like they owned the place so it was a little hard to tell who was really in charge. Everyone in the club seemed to know them and wanted to hang out with them, especially with Frank. They all catered a bit more to him. It turned out that Frank owns the place. After a while, he approached me and we started talking. I told him how fly he looked and he told me I could have the same things he had if I didn't mind a little risk, as in getting my hands dirty, was how he put it, and it went from there. His club is the biggest secret in town. Not many people know of his connection with the club. He's got other businesses I hear but he runs the drugs out of the club. Got it set up all slick and shit."

Jordan sat facing her sister. She wasn't sure how involved Steffie was with Frank's business, but she knew it wasn't good. And, seeing the overwrought condition she was in, Jordan decided not to go after her too harshly.

"That son of a bitch," Stevie hissed. "I knew he was doing some things, big things, but I had no idea he was rolling like that and there is no way did I think he'd ever involve my sister in his shit."

"I did question some of the things he was doing but he managed to sidestep it or would give me an answer that appeared plausible. I never thought he was dealing in drugs nor did I know he had any connection with a nightclub." Jordan sighed deeply. "I blame myself for some of this. I promised you guys that I would take care of you until you were able to take care of yourselves and I can see I've failed miserably."

"Stop talking like that, Jordan," Stevie said. "You haven't failed anyone. You have been more than a sister to Steffie and me. You've been more like a mother and we appreciate you."

"Don't blame yourself for this. None of what I did is your fault," Steffie said. "All this is on me, always wanting everything immediately, not wanting to wait.

"You know, I had always pride myself on knowing people but I was so far off on this one. If I didn't have my head stuck so far up Frank's ass, I wouldn't have missed all the signs that I missed," Jordan said, rubbing the side of her head. "Mrs. Irene was right. Love can surely blind a person."

"Mrs. Irene?" Stevie asked.

"That another story," Jordan said.

"I'm no longer involved with the drugs," Steffie informed them, then she fell silent.

Jordan and Stevie cast each other a look. Then Jordan said, "There's something else going on with you. What is it, Steffie?"

Steffie remained silent.

Stevie turned so he could look his twin sister in her eyes. "What are you not telling us, Steffie?"

Then, unexpectedly, Steffie began to cry.

"Steffie, what's going on?" Jordan asked. "Talk to us, please."

"I'm pregnant," the usually calm Steffie said, and she broke down sobbing.

"What?" Jordan stiffened. She was incredulous, tugging at her ear lobe.

"Fuck?" Stevie leaped from his seat.

Steffie was crying uncontrollable now and Jordan and Steven went to her and consoled her until she was able to speak again. And, she did so without prompting. "About a month ago I went over to Frank's Club to do a pick up. His people told me he was at the shop so I went there. He was alone. He offered me a drink, I accepted and that was the last thing I remembered."

Jordan and Stevie both had the look of horror on their faces. "What do you mean?" Jordan asked.

"I woke up the next morning in bed with Frank, we were both naked," Steffie said.

"What?" Stevie punched his fist in his hand.

Jordan screeched in disgust. "That no good son of a bitch." Then, she asked, "Why didn't you come to us?"

"I was ashamed of what happened to me, what I'd done."

"We're family. We're all we've got and we're always gonna stick together, Twin. You know that," Stevie said, turned and headed towards the door.

"Where are you going?" Jordan asked.

"I'm gonna have a talk with Frank."

"Hold up, I'm going with you," Jordan said, then she looked at Steffie. "Will you be alright here until we get back?"

"No, I'm going with you," Steffie answered, and together, the three of them left Jordan's house.

It didn't take long for Stevie to reach Frank's Welding Shop. Through the window, they could see Frank sitting on top of his desk with his legs crossed, laughing and talking on the phone. They got out of the car and walked up to the door. Steffie walked in first. Frank turned to see who'd entered his shop. "Steffie, I knew you'd be back." His face held a look of triumphant satisfaction. "So what are you doing here? You wanna get back in the game?" He asked, a huge smile on his face.

When Jordan and Stevie walked in, his mouth fell open in surprise. His smile faded but was replaced by a smirk.

Jordan looked at Frank through slanted eyes. Stevie tried to walk past Jordan to Frank but without removing her eyes from Frank's, she placed her hand against her brother's chest for him to remain in place.

"You think you're slick, getting my sister involved with drugs," Jordan said.

"I didn't force her to take the job. I asked if she was interested in doing some runs for me, I told her what she could make. She loves money, she accepted the job and here we are. Steffie is a big girl. In fact, she's a grown woman now and free to make her own decisions, or haven't you two noticed?"

Jordan went on as if Frank hadn't spoken. "When I threw your ass out of my house and told you I never wanted to see you again, you told me I'd be sorry about that decision. So this is what you meant? You intended to exact your revenge against me by doing what you did to my sister? You already had her running drugs for you but that wasn't enough. You took your revenge further by raping her." She scowled at him. All the while Stevie was fuming; his face contorted and his fingers were balled up into huge fists.

Frank looked from Jordan ice cold eyes to Steven's deadly glare, but he didn't comment to that.

"Do you know she's pregnant?!"

Frank got up from sitting on his desk and walked around and stood behind the desk. His deep set dark eyes suddenly shifted from Jordan to Steffie, then back to Jordan.

"If she is pregnant, you can't blame me. Besides, there's no proof that I'm the daddy. I was there. Sure, I tasted what she had to offer, but I wasn't the only one. That little sister of yours is cut from a different cloth than you. The night Steffie spent here, a lot of guys got a piece of that sweet tender action," Frank sneered. Those were the last words that came out of his mouth before Stevie, eyes blazing, rushed out of Jordan's reach before she could stop him, and he yanked Frank from behind his desk, dragged him across the desk and slammed him against a wall. Frank had always prided himself on his physique, his military background, and how he'd intimidated many people in the past by his size and muscular built, but he was no match for Stevie who punched Frank in his face twice and blood shot from his nose. He picked Frank up in the air, slammed him down, hard and when Frank landed on the floor, Stevie straddled him and shoved his fist into Frank's face several times, turning it into a bloody mess.

Jordan and Steffie managed to pull Stevie off of Frank and begged him to stop. Well, there was no fight. Stevie whupped Frank's ass. Plain and simple. Had Jordan and Steffie not stopped Stevie, he would've brought much greater harm to Frank. He hit Frank once more before he got off of him and said, "If you come near my sisters again, either one of them, I will kill you, mother fucker. That's a guarantee," Stevie swore, shaking his fist at Frank.

Frank had wronged people, many of them had scores to settle with him so Stevie was the last person he wanted to come after him again.

"I've got information on you, Frank and if come near my family again, your ass is grass," Jordan said, then to her siblings, she said, "Let's get out of here."

"Yeah," Steffie said, stepping across Frank who was still sprawled out on the floor. "We've done here."

The three of them left Frank groaning in a bloody heap on the floor.

Arriving back at Jordan's house, they went into the kitchen and sat at the table. Jordan looked at Stevie's hands and saw that one was bloody. "Do you think your hand is broken?" She asked, as she examined it.

"A little sore but it's alright," he replied.

Jordan left the kitchen and returned with a towel, first aid kit and alcohol to take care of Stevie's hand.

"We should run by the Emergency Room and have them check it to make sure it's not broken."

"Naah." He moved his fingers around. "It's not broken. It'll be alright in a couple of days."

"You sure beat the hell out of Frank," Steffie said and chuckled. Jordan and Stevie gave her a look. "Well, you did."

"She's right," Jordan said. "I thought we would go there and talk to him, but you put hands on that boy. He deserved it. He might come after you. Frank is dirty dog. There's no way to tell what he might do."

Stevie snorted dismissively. "He's also a coward. He doesn't want any part of me."

"He thought his military training was everything. I mean that training is great but he didn't know Stevie has had Martial Arts training from the time he was a kid, earned all those belts, and taught the sport to help earn his way through college," Steffie said and added, "No, he doesn't want anything else to do with Stevie. That's for sure."

The three of them chuckled.

When Jordan had finished with Stevie's hand and put the first-aid items away, she removed hot dogs from the refrigerator and put them into a pot of water that she set on

204

the stove to heat up, she took chips from the cabinet and within minutes, they were eating hot dogs and potato chips and drinking beer. Jordan asked, "Any thoughts about the baby?"

Steffie replied, "I can't talk about that tonight. I promise I will but not tonight."

"We'll talk about it soon," Stevie said.

"Yes. Soon," Steffie answered, sadly.

When they finished eating, they talked at the table while Jordan went through the mail that Stevie had brought in and placed on the table. She picked up a letter, looked at it and smiled. "This is from Brad," she said. She opened the envelope and was stunned when a check fell from the letter onto the table. She picked up the check and looked at it. "What is this?" She said in almost a whisper. She placed the check back on the table and read the letter out loud.

'Hey guys,
Hope you all are good. Sorry I hadn't been in touch in a while. I want to thank you again for everything. Jordan, Mama always had faith in your fashion interests and wanted to help a little. I hope this small check will assist. Please let know if there is ever anything I

can do for either of you.
Take care, you guys and
much love.

     Brad.'

 Steffie picked up the check, looked at it, then pushed it across the table to Stevie. "That was so nice of Mrs. Irene," she said.

 "Yes it was," Stevie agreed.

 "That's a huge check too," Steffie said, looking at the check.

 "I never expected anything, but it is so like Mrs. Irene to do something like this." Jordan brushed away a tear. "She was one of the nicest and most unselfish persons that I've ever known, and I miss her so much."

 Steffie replied, "I know. So do I."

 Jordan felt a sudden chill in the air. She got up, adjusted the thermostat and returning to her seat at the table and said, "Why don't you guys spend the night? We can talk and enjoy each other's company."

 "Works for me," Stevie replied.

 "Sure," Steffie said. "It'll be like old times."

 After a while, Steffie got up and went to the bathroom. She returned a short time later, looking relieved and announced, "I'm not pregnant."

"What happened?" Jordan asked, going over to Steffie.

"I got my period. I was probably late because of the stress I was under working for Frank. I don't know, but I feel fine."

"Get your coat. I'm taking you to the Emergency Room," Jordan said.

"No. We don't need to do that. I'm good. I got frightened because I'm almost never late but I do remember my Freshman year in college when I got all worked up just before Finals and I was late. I was about two weeks late that time also but my period came and I was fine. Same thing this time."

"I think it would be a good idea if you get checked out anyway. There's just no way to tell what happened at Frank's that night, so to be sure, let's get checked out."

"Good idea," Stevie said.

Steffie is stubborn and it took a while for them to convince her to get a check-up, but she finally agreed for Jordan to take her to the doctor the following day. Jordan tugged at her earlobe and began clearing the table. Then, they got up from the table, went to the living room and settled down to watch an episode of Martin. Stevie looked over at Jordan. "Stop tugging that earlobe before you pop that thing off," he said and laughed.

"She still does that," Steffie said. "Momma said as a child, when Jordan got upset, she would tug at her ear."

"Some things never change," Jordan grinned.

Before going to sleep, she called Toby and told him what happened, including Mrs. Irene's gift to her.

"Is everything alright?" He asked.

"Everything's fine."

"What about you? Are you alright?" He wanted to know.

"I'm fine, sweetie. How are you doing?"

"Other than missing you, I'm fine. I should be there with you," he said.

"I'm fine but I thank you for thinking of me that way. I miss you."

"I miss you too," Toby said, then asked, "When are you coming to see me again? Soon, I hope."

"You know you can come see me anytime you want."

"But I've got something here I'd like to show you, and I can't wait to see you again."

"I can't wait to see you also," she said softly and sweetly.

"If you keep talking like that, I will be on the road, heading your way in a flash."

"You're crazy. You know that, right?"

"Crazy about you, Miss Banks, and if I had one wish, you'd be in this bed with me."

"Soon, my darling. Soon," she said and she meant it. She just wished she could erase the sadness from his eyes.

The following day, Jordan called the doctor and scheduled an appointment for Steffie. Two days later, they went to see the doctor who ordered a number of tests that revealed Steffie wasn't pregnant, no STDs, she was in good health.

CHAPTER 19

After work on Friday, Jordan flew to Atlanta to see Toby. The sight of him, when he met her at the airport, sent her heart racing out of control, to the point where she thought she was going to faint.

Jordan dropped her carry-on bag and ran into Toby's arms. He lifted her up and twirled her around. Neither could believe they were seeing each other, were in each other's arms again. Still in his arms, her feet not touching the ground, he looked into her eyes and said, "Hey you."

"Hey you."

Toby kissed Jordan. When he released her, they left the airport. Soon Jordan and Toby were at his house. After putting down her suitcase, Toby pulled Jordan to him and their bodies collided together. Her arms went up around his neck as his arms coiled around her waist in a steel grip, binding her to him. Then, his mouth came crushing down to take hers in a kiss that sent shivers down her spine, a kiss of mind-blowing hunger.

With their bodies pressed close together, their tongues danced, explored, demanded. The chemistry between Jordan and Toby was electric, the way it had been from the day they met. When he broke the kiss and pulled back to look into her eyes, he was surprised to see she'd been crying. "Why are you crying, baby?" He cupped her face in his hands.

"I can't believe we're together, and I'm so happy." She sobbed against his shoulder.

Toby swept Jordan up into his arms and kissing her passionately, he carried her to his bedroom where they removed their clothes.

On the bed, her legs fell apart and when he touched her at her most intimate spot, he was mindful she was already wet for him. She reached out, gripped his naked buttocks and drew him between her legs. Then and there, they made love, and it was like nothing either had ever experienced.

Later as they lay together, he said, "Remember the very first time when I visited you and you asked why I hadn't gotten in touch with you? And this is no excuse but do you remember that?"

"Yes."

"You remember what I told you?"

"Yes."

"I told you I was busy, right?"

"What are you getting at?"

Toby repeated the question, "I told you I was busy..... right?"

"Yes."

He released her to walk over to the night table where he removed a document from the top drawer and with a secretive smile, he handed the document to her.

"What is this?" She asked, a puzzled expression on her face, taking the document from his outstretched hand. She looked to him for answers.

"Look at it."

She opened the document, read it and the puzzled expression on her face deepened. After reading the document, she raised her eyes and looked questioningly at him. "This is a Purchase Agreement and it has my name on it." She paused a second. "It looks like I'm a property own here. Am I the owner of property here in Atlanta?"

"Yes. You own property here in the city, downtown Atlanta. This property is yours. I purchased it for you."

"What does this mean?"

"You are now the owner of this piece of property and you're free to do whatever you want with it. I was thinking you could turn it into a daycare center, a nightclub." His smile broadened as he added, "or you could turn it into a design house. Of course, that's up to you. It's your space."

One of Jordan's hands went up to cover her mouth while the document shook in the other hand. She looked at Toby, a hesitant smile tugged her lips as she tugged at her ear lobe. "Toby, you didn't."

"I did."

"I don't believe this." She went into his arms, her eyes bright with tears. She lay the document on the bed, took Toby's face in both hands and she kissed him softly, gently. When the kiss ended, they sat on the bed together. He spread the document out on the bed, and showed Jordan the layout of the newly acquired property.

"This could be the sewing area or that area, if you prefer," he said, pointing a finger to the plan.

"Yeah," she said, excitedly. "And, right there by the windows, will be my office and this area will be the supply room." Jordan looked at Toby, leaned over, kissed him and shaking her head in disbelief, she held the document against her chest. "I don't believe it. I'm gonna have my own design house."

"I can show you the property anytime you want." He tried not to show it but his excitement perfectly matched hers.

Excited with anticipation, they dressed, he drove to the warehouse and parked near the front door. "Is that it?" She asked.

"Yep."

"It is huge."

Toby smiled. They buttoned up their coats, got out of the car and with their arms wrapped around each other, they walked up to the door. "It's gonna be cold in there because the heat isn't on yet."

"I'm so excited," she said, barely able to restrain herself from leaping in the air.

He opened the door, hit the ON switch and flooded the space with light.

"Oh my God, this is incredible." She couldn't restrain herself this time. She screamed, leaped in the air and wrapped her arms around Toby. At a glance, she could see endless possibilities. She released him and whirled around taking it all in.

"What are you thinking?" He asked, arms folded across his chest.

She turned to look at him. "I see not only fitting rooms, design tables and seamstresses working in here, I imagine phones ringing nonstop of course with lots of orders coming in."

CHAPTER 20

Jordan and Toby were very excited as they walked through the building, giving it a once over. As they made their way back to the entry door, she looked into his eyes and asked, "Toby, I'm not dreaming, am I? You really did buy this place for me, didn't you."

"This is all yours to do with as you please."

"I can believe someone like you exist. You're such a wonderful man."

"You deserve so much, baby. I'm just happy I can play a small part in you getting some of what you want."

"Thank you so much."

"You are welcome, but right now, I want to get you home. It's cold in here, and I don't want you to get sick again."

Jordan liked the sound of that. He was gonna take her home. She knew she was reading much more into it than was meant but she liked the sound of it anyway.

"Thank you, and I promise, I'm gonna

pay you back?"

"Sweetheart, there's no paying me back. This is me trying to help make your dream come true. I want you to be happy. That's all the payment I need."

"I love you."

"I love you.

Then, grinning, with their hands locked, they rushed out of the building, got into the car and headed home. As he drove through the busy traffic, Toby looked over at Jordan, feeling the electricity between them mount. He leaned towards her, reached around her shoulders, and pulling her closer to him, he ran his hand inside her bra to caress her breast. At the same time, her hand went inside his pants and massaged his hardened member. As she stroked him, his member grew harder. Toby pressed down hard on the accelerator. He wanted to get Jordan home as soon as possible.

Arriving home, they quickly exited the car and raced into the house, tearing off their clothing as they went. In the kitchen, Toby pulled Jordan into his arms and kissed her passionately. In an instance they were against the table. Toby used one hand to clear items from the table before he lifted her onto the table. Then he kissed her again

217

as he wedged himself between her thighs. He thrust his harden member into her wet slit. Once inside, he pulled her hips to the edge of the table where he held her captive and ground into her. He moved in and out of her. As she arched her body and moved hard against him, his movements quickened and he plunged into her with all the passion he possessed. He slammed into her one last time with her crying out at the most intense orgasm she'd ever experienced.

Later in bed, Toby said, "I've never felt this way before. You make me feel so much. I can't even describe it. You do things to me that I can't even pronounce."

That brought a little smile to Jordan's face. "That's exactly how I feel."

"Jordan, I want you. I want to laugh with you when you laugh, cry with you when you hurt, fight for you all the time, and die for you, if necessary."

"Umm," she moaned. She'd never felt more love in her heart for Toby than she'd come close to feeling for anyone before. He brought so much to her life and she knew with every fiber of her being that she'd spend the rest of her life appreciating and loving that man.

After a while, she said, "Toby, I owe you so much."

"No, you don't."

"Please, just listen to me for a minute. You, Toby, you! You made me laugh at a time when laughter was the farthest thing from my mind. You made me feel better about myself when I was in so much pain that I didn't know where I could put that pain or whether I would ever get over that hurt. But you, your kindness did something that I didn't even think was possible. You made me feel whole again. You brought me through it all. And, as if those things weren't enough, you fell in love with me." She placed both hands against her chest. "Yes! You fell in love with me!"

Toby had given her so much. She wanted to give him something back. She knew he was in love with her and he knew she was in love with him. She knew her love made Toby happy only his eyes still held sadness that appear to run deep. "Can we talk?" She asked.

"Sure."

"Can we talk about your mother?!"

Toby looked at Jordan with a furrow in his brow. "My mother?"

"Talk to me about her."

Toby was quiet for a moment.

"My mother and I were close. Very close. I suppose as close as a mother and son could be and when she died, the loss took a toll on me."

"I can see your pain, Toby. Not only is it etched in your face, I see it in your eyes."

"The pain is real all right."

"Losing a loved one is tragic, I know."

"Losing a loving parent is one of the most difficult things one can overcome."

"Yes, and when something like that happens, all that hurt, all that pain, I do know we have to find a place to put that pain. One thing we have to do is face it and release it." She paused a moment before she asked, "You haven't cried for that tragic loss, the loss of your mother? Have you?"

Toby's head snapped in Jordan's direction. "Cried?!"

"Yes! Why haven't you cried for your loss? For your mother?"

"I told you how I feel about that."

"I know but I need you to do what is necessary for you, what you must do for you."

"My mother always taught me to be strong, and I've always wanted to be strong for her."

"I'm sure you were strong for her. Sometimes crying shows more strength than restraint."

"Why are we talking about this? My mother," Toby began and the sadness etched its way deeper into the crevices of his face, "is dead, it was a terrible loss, I'll always feel that loss and that's that."

Each was quiet for a moment. Then, she said, "It's okay, you know!"

"What?!" Toby turned and looked at her.

"It's okay to cry for your mother. Crying doesn't mean that you're weak. Quite the contrary. Crying shows compassion, that you have a heart, that you feel—deeply." She opened her arms to him. "Come here. Come here, baby. I'm here for you. Please let me be here for you. Let me help you."

"I don't need to cry."

Jordan pulled him to her so that his head rested against her chest. She held him there.

"I don't want to cry."

Jordan continued to hold him close.

"I don't want to….," he began and as though the flood gates opened, his sobs erupted, and his entire body shook as he released the pain that had been holding him prisoner for what appeared a very long time.

Jordan held him, gently swaying back and forth, comforting him as he wept.

"Let it go, baby. Let it all out. I love you. I will always love you. Sometimes we have to find a way to release so that we can be healthy and move forward. Let it out. Let it out. I love you so much." As Jordan consoled the man she loved, tears also rolled down her cheeks.

After a while, he said, "I haven't cried since I was a child."

Jordan held his face in her hands and kissed the tears from his cheeks. "I love you," she said, softly but her heart wanted to scream those words, and she dissolve into his chest.

"I love you."

Lying in his arms sometime later, Jordan said, "Remember I told you I bought you a Christmas present?"

"Yes, you did say that, didn't you?"

She reached over to the night table, picked up a box and handed it to him. It's just a little sumphin sumphin."

"Thank you, baby. Now, let's see what we've got here," he said, accepting the present and began tearing into it. He took the photo album and began flipping through the pages. He was surprised and happy to see photographs of him and Jordan as well as the new friends they met in Montego Bay. "Ahh, this is great. That's a great one right there also," he said of a picture of the six of them at the mall in Jamaica. After viewing the last page in the album, he closed it and placed it on the night table. He changed the subject. "I'd like to meet your family; your sister and brother. I'd like to get to know them."

Jordan smiled. Steffie had moved into Mrs. Irene's house across the street and Stevie was back and forth from where he worked in Orlando.

"I would love that. We can definitely make that happen."

CHAPTER 21

Alternating weekly visits and holidays, Jordan and Toby saw each other and when she was in Atlanta, she and Toby supervised the conversion of the warehouse into a workable space for Jordan's new design house; a large space for cutting and sewing, a fitting area, receptionist area, offices, rest rooms and a small conference room.

It had been obvious that Toby had listened to everything Jordan told him when they were in Jamaica and he remembered. The building he secured for her provided everything that Jordan wanted and needed to pursue her life goal as a designer. She was happy. She was in love with the most wonderful man in the world and amazingly, he loved her back. And not only did Toby loved her, he respected what she wanted to do with her life, and he wanted to assist her in realizing her goals. He supported her completely! Her future looked bright. Her life was perfect.

One weekend Toby picked Jordan up at the airport, drove her to his house and when they entered, immediately Jordan noticed that other than the portrait of his mother that hung over the mantle, there was one other picture of her and him on a table in the den. When Jordan asked about the missing photos, Toby explained. "When you and I were looking through the album with the pictures of all of us in Montego Bay, it gave me an idea."

"It did?"

"I put most of the pictures in albums. I'll always have them and can look at them whenever I want." He smiled at her. "I know you left the extra albums on purpose and I appreciate it."

As she smiled back at him, she noticed his eyes no longer held that deep sadness that was evident even when he was happy.

On Toby's visit to Augusta, he met Stevie and Steffie. The four of them had breakfast at Sue's Kitchen, one of Jordan and the twins' favorite eating place. All through breakfast, Jordan and the twins told stories about them growing up and he shared his upbringing as well. She could see that the three liked each other and when they left the restaurant, Steffie had insisted that Toby and Jordan come over for dinner on one of his trips to Augusta. Toby was happy to oblige, and Stevie and Toby agreed to hoop up for a game of basketball.

Later that day, Jordan introduced Toby to Maggie and Samantha and that evening the three couples went out for drinks and dancing, and Toby was a hit. Maggie didn't pass up the opportunity to tell Jordan she thought Toby was definitely a keeper.

After two nights of passionate love making and exploring and learning even more about each other, early Monday morning, Jordan drove Toby to the Airport, and he took a flight back to Atlanta.

It was Friday, the last weekend in April. Toby flew in to Augusta, Jordan picked him up at the airport. It'd been a week since they last saw each other but it seemed like a lifetime. The more Jordan got to know Toby, the more she wanted to know and the more she loved him for what she already knew. She missed him terribly when they weren't together.

She entered the airport and it wasn't long before she saw Toby with a carry-on bag, coming towards her. When he saw her, his face broke into a wide grin as did hers. She rushed to him, he drew her into him arms and they shared a kiss.

When they broke the kiss, she leaned away from him and looked into his eyes. "Hey you," she said.

"Hey you," he replied.

On the way to her house, Toby insisted they stop at a grocery store to pick up a few items for him to cook for dinner.

Arriving home, Jordan and Toby carried everything inside. "Would you like me to show you where everything is; pots, pans?"

"No, you go on and do what you need to do. I know my way around a kitchen fairly well. I should be able to find what I need."

While Toby was in the kitchen making dinner for them, Jordan slipped into a pair of jeans and a blouse, and she went into the sewing room to work with fabrics and patterns. She smiled, hearing the sound of pots and pans banging in the kitchen. Less than two hours later, he set the table and called Jordan in for dinner.

"You set a really nice table," she said.

"I do okay. I hope you enjoy what I've prepared for us."

"Whatever it is, it smells terrific."

Once seated across from each other, they chatted over broiled steaks, mashed potatoes with brown gravy, grilled parmesan broccoli and a carrot salad. Later, they shared a dish of chocolate ice cream for dessert. After dinner, with glasses of wine in their hands, Jordan and Toby moved to the couch in the living room where they listened to popular jazz music playing in the background. Suddenly, the doorbell rang. She answered to find Stevie and Steffie standing there.

"What are you two doing here?" Jordan asked, and stepped back for them to enter.

"Toby asked us to come by. You guys are okay?" Stevie wanted to know.

"Yeah, we're fine. I didn't know Toby asked you two to come by," Jordan said. "You want a drink?" She offered.

"Yeah, that sounds great," Stevie replied.

"A glass of wine would be nice," Steffie answered.

Jordan went into the kitchen, poured a drink for Steffie and Stevie and returned to the living room.

When they were all seated, Toby said,

"Steffie and Steven, I suppose you're wondering why I asked you to come here tonight. I know you two don't know me very well but I'm hoping that will change." He paused a moment, before saying, "and we can become family."

Steffie's hands went up to her mouth. Stevie's eyes left Toby and went to Jordan who looked as though she was in shock.

"What are you talking about, Toby," Jordan asked.

Toby knew what he wanted and it was Jordan. He wanted to be with her, take care of her. He wanted to please her more than any woman he'd ever met, and he intended to do just that. Those feelings weren't new to him. He hadn't known Jordan very long, but he was certain of his feelings. He was more certain of that than he'd been of anything in his life.

Toby directed his comments to Stevie and Steffie. "I'm in love with your sister, I want to be able to wake up with her in the morning, every morning, and I'm asking you two for your sister's hand in marriage. I want Jordan to marry me."

"What?" Jordan's fingers went to her ear lobe as her eyes widened in shocked surprise. She was far more affected by Toby's revelation than the twins.

Stevie was the first of the twins to speak. "Well," he cleared his throat, "I know my sister loves you and I know you make her happier than I've ever seen her and if you love her as much as I think you do, then you have my blessing. It'll be cool having you become a part of our family."

Steffie leaped from her seat and ran to Jordan, pulled her from the couch, and they embraced. Jordan was trembling.

"What about you, Steffie?" Toby asked.

Steffie said, "Yes! Yes! Yes!" She released her sister, went to Toby and hugged him. "I expected something like this to happen. My sister is such a great gal, and she deserves a wonderful man like you. And, just so you know, this family looks out for each other so you had better take good care of this lady, you hear?"

"I absolutely will," Toby assured them.

Steffie turned back to Jordan. "Congrats, sis, I'm so happy for both of you." Then Steffie whispered in Jordan's ear, "I know he hasn't asked *you* yet, but he will." Then to her brother, "Come on, let's get out of here and let these two celebrate."

After Steffie and Steven left, pulling a small white box from his pants pocket and getting down on one knee, Toby looked at Jordan. "I surprised you, didn't I?!"

"Yes you did!"

"So, what is your answer? Will you marry me?"

Jordan looked down into the face of the man she loved with all of her heart and replied, "Yes, baby! Yes! I will marry you."

Toby removed a 2ct Round Halo engagement ring from the box and placed it on Jordan's finger. He stood up and they sealed his question and her response with a kiss. When they pulled apart, he said, "You know you had to accept my proposal, huh? After all, I was winning three to one." They chuckled. Jordan pulled Toby's face down to meet her. They kissed again. This time, it was even more passionate, explosive. He then carried her off to bed.

Jordan and Toby were asleep in her bed. She woke up, looked at Toby and feeling jolts of excitement racing through her body, she ran a hand across his face. She threw back the covers and eased out of bed. She got on her knees and closed her eyes in preparation for her daily morning prayers.

"God, I thank You for Your goodness and mercy, I thank You for everyone and everything you put into my life, and I thank You for turning my entire life around." She continued to pray and among the people she mentioned, her siblings, Mrs. Irene and Toby were included. She ended her prayer and still on her knees, whispered, "You were so right, Mrs. Irene. You were right about everything. Thank you. I love you, and I miss you so much."

Jordan opened her eyes. Seeing that Toby was still asleep, she got up from the floor, pick up her phone from the night table, and she went into the living room where she plopped down on the couch and excitedly placed a conference call to Maggie and Samantha with the good news. After receiving elated congratulations, she sat there alone for a few minutes, thinking about how different her life was then as opposed to how it was even a year ago. Jordan raised her left hand and stared admiringly at the diamond that had made its home on her ring finger. She knew she'd cherish that ring and the man who gave it to her for all time.

A jolt of excitement ran the course of Jordan's body. Not only was her mind still reeling from the events from last night, more than anything, her heart was racing out of control. She took a deep breath and looked up towards the ceiling. She was engaged! Engaged to the man she loved! She was engaged to Toby!

Jordan got up from the couch, returned to her bedroom and eased into bed with Toby.

"I missed you," he said, wrapping his arms around her, snuggling closely to her.

"I'm back now and I'll be here with you forever."

"That sounds perfect."

Snuggling together, Jordan had never been happier, neither was Toby. Then, they slept.

At the end of the school term, Jordan resigned her position at the high school, they threw her a going away party; her siblings and Toby were there for the special occasion and there were some tearful goodbyes. The following day, Jordan and Toby drove to Atlanta and her new home.

On July 5th, Jordan and Toby got married in a small but beautiful rooftop ceremony at the beautiful and elegant Queen Plaza Hotel in Atlanta, followed by a lovely reception with a five piece live band that played some oldies but goodies as well as current popular tunes. Samantha served as Jordan's Matron of Honor and Steffie and Maggie were Maids of Honor. The day after the wedding, Jordan and Toby flew to Montego Bay. They could have gone anywhere on their honeymoon but they chose Montego Bay because of all it represented for them. And, the two weeks they spent on the island were just as magical and special as the day they met. The two could not have been happier.

Toby showed Jordan around Atlanta and introduced her to more of his friends and business associates.

Less than a year after their wedding, Jordan hired office staff, seamstress, she purchased furniture, sewing machines, fabrics and other supplies and equipment to stock the new business. One night as Jordan and Toby lay in bed together, he said, "You haven't said anything about the name of your business. Have you decided?"

"Yes. As you know, my label is Jordan Dakota Banks, but the name of the design house will be named something special to both of us."

"Really? What is it?"

"A Day in Paradise," Jordan whispered.

"A Day in Paradise," Toby whispered back. "I like that. I like it a lot."

"Then that'll be the name of our new business. A Day in Paradise."

They sealed their decision with a kiss and on December 31, the following year and Jordan's birthday, she cut the ribbon at *A Day in Paradise Fashions,* and later, she premiered her first fashion line. She was excited. Many wonderful things were happening in her life, all at the same time. There had been such a demand on her time that she hadn't had time to talk to her husband. She was so grateful for him for so many reasons, and she wanted to tell him.

There was a crowd in attendance, a good amount of press was there, and the guests ate hors d'oeuvres, drank champagne and mingled while hundreds of orders were taken by Jordan's staff.

When Trish and Jim entered the design house, Jordan and Trish squealed with delight at seeing each other. As they released each other, Trish said, "Darling, I'm sorry we couldn't make the wedding but Jim and I were at his mother's funeral."

"I know," Jordan said and expressed sympathy to them on his loss.

"Gina and Martin probably won't be attending," Trish mentioned.

Jordan and Trish made a face and Jordan said, sadly, "Yeah."

Holding a glass of fruit punch in her hand, Jordan mingled with her guests and shared some of her plans for her business. After a while, she looked across the crowded room at Toby and caught his eye. He looked relaxed and happy and that happiness blazed in his eye that no longer held the sadness they had when they met. She smiled at him, her eyes sparkling with her own happiness. He smiled back at her. She could see his love for her shining in his eyes and he could see hers as well. Their love was real and it was there for the world to see.

A short time later, Toby walked up to her, placed an arm around her waist and kissed her on her lips. "I'm so proud of you, baby. Are you enjoying what you've created here?"

"I'm thrilled." Jordan looked around. beaming. "I'm so please with what is happening. For so long, this was only a dream and now because of you, today, it is a reality." Turning happy eyes to her husband, she said, "Thank you, Toby. Thank you so much."

236

"No thanks is necessary, sweetie. You had a dream and you believed in that dream. That's all it takes to have a dream grow into a future. I'm just happy that you are living the dream you've had most of your life, and I want to say congratulations to you, baby. I'm so happy to be here to witness this with you," he said, spreading his hands around the room. Just enjoy every moment of it."

"Your participation was huge, baby. This wouldn't have happened without you."

"Okay, I assisted with the space, but you were on your way to doing this yourself. I expedited one step. In any event, I don't want you to wear yourself out because you still have an event to take care of tonight. Your husband." He gave her a sexy smile.

"I'm gonna be more than pleased to take care of you, husband."

"Thank you, wife."

Toby took Jordan's glass from her hand and took a sip. He made a face. "Punch." He handed her glass back to her.

"Yes."

"You don't want anything stronger? A glass of champagne, perhaps? After all, this is a very special night for you."

"This is fine." She smiled and took a sip. "I've got a question for you."

"Sure, baby. Anything."

"What would you think about converting one of our bedrooms into a nursery?"

"That is our home. You can make any changes you want." Then, realizing her meaning, a combination of disbelief and happiness, covering his face, he slowly asked, "What are you saying? Are you saying we're…..?" He paused.

"Yes! We're gonna have a baby!"

"Are you serious?"

"Yes, honey. I'm absolutely serious."

Toby lifted her up, twirled her around and kissed her. He released her and got down on his knees before her.

"What are you doing?" She asked.

Never taking his eyes from hers, he placed both hands on her stomach and he kissed it. "You have no idea how happy you've made me." He kissed her stomach once more before he stood up.

Jordan lay her head against Toby's chest, she closed her eyes and sighed deeply. "I've never been happier in my entire life."

"Your happiness means everything to me."

When the event ended, Toby drove them home. On the way, she said, "I've gotta call Steffie, Stevie, Maggie and Samantha and tell them our wonderful news."

"They're gonna be stoked."

"I know. I will call others tomorrow."

"Sounds good. I want you to rest."

She smiled over at him. "I will."

They entered the house and after they were in comfortable clothes, sitting on the couch in front of a fire in the fireplace, in each other's arms, it begun to rain.

Jordan got up, walked over and touched a control button on the wall that opened the drapes, exposing a wall of windows. She stood there and stared out at the rain. In the next minute, Toby was at her side, and he slid his arm around her waist.

"I know what you are thinking," he said.

"I know," she replied, snuggling closer to him, with the memory of the day they met floating through her mind.

"Happy?"

"Very happy."

He placed his free hand on her stomach and closed his eyes as he gently stroked her stomach, filled with joy knowing that a part of him was growing inside her. She heard a soft mourn escaped him as he drew her closer.

Then, she said softly, "I love you, baby."

Toby opened his eyes and looked down into his wife's beautiful eyes, the eyes of the woman he loved more than life, the woman who made him happier than he ever thought was possible. "I love you more," he replied, and he never meant anything more in his entire life.